It says here you shot a puppy.

For Sarah, who has no idea how much I appreciate her.

I) ....and so it begins.

"It says here you shot a puppy. You were sitting in your house and leaned out the window with a .22 and shot a five week old Bulldog puppy in the backside. Also says you confessed to doing it. Is that true?"

I expected the client to shift around in her seat, maybe mumble some kind of denial or at least start explaining herself or something. What I got was a casual affirmation, as if I was asking her to confirm her address. Here this person was charged with shooting a puppy (discharge of a firearm near a house and cruelty to animals to be exact) and she is just looking at me like she wonders what the problem is.

I first was assigned this case about a week ago, it was just another in a large pile of petty criminal cases assigned to me by the judge. More accurately they were assigned to the Public Defender office, but these were my share of the burden. Hidden among the usual slew of drunken driving and domestic violence cases was this little oddity. Just the normal peculiar police prose saying that she had shot a puppy. It described the gun, the yard, and the dog in detail. It also told the narrative about how the officer received a complaint from a neighbor, was advised that the suspect had wounded the dog with a firearm, and also mentioned that the suspect had admitted to shooting the dog.

What it didn't contain was a single clue as to why the dog had been shot. None. While I was in deepest West Virginia, it wasn't like people went around popping puppies with low-caliber rifles. Just like in any other impoverished area there was of course a level of crime. Drunken driving, bar fights, forgery, burglary, and perhaps the occasional child molestation were to be expected, but this? The client was scheduled to come in to discuss the matter on Tuesday, so I also had the anticipation of knowing I would have some idea of what was going on at that point. The curiosity was killing me. I had handled and was handling various major felonies, some of which were both high profile and controversial, but something about the puppy shooting

IT SAYS HERE...

bugged me. What possible explanation could there be? I had defended some pretty seemingly awful acts before, and could with a straight face argue some kind of justification or at least mitigation for the action, but shooting a puppy.

So, there I am in my office, talking to this lady.

"So you are admitting to shooting this puppy? Why did you shoot it?"

"I was trying to protect it. It was going to get hurt."

This was unexpected. My mind reeled, but the first rule of interviewing a client is to get the information. Try to keep an open mind. I tried not to sound too shocked. "You shot the puppy to protect it? From what?"

"The pit bulls I had in my yard. I have these pit bulls tied up in front of my door to keep my bastard ex-boyfriend out of the house. I seen that there puppy wandering over towards my dogs and I don't think I'd have liked to see it get all chewed up, so I shot a warning shot but it just kept coming. So I tried to hit it in the ass. I reckoned that the poor thing had a better chance with the gunshot wound than if my dogs got a hold of it. Stupid neighbors know I had the dogs and everything, but they let a puppy wander around? You'd think they'd be in trouble for being that stupid."

7

IT SAYS HERE...

The lady further explained how her violent idiot boyfriend would call and threaten to sneak into the house and beat her up, The cops couldn't protect her so they advised her to get a dog.

There can always be a good reason. Or at least one that sounds good. At the hearing the owners of the puppy showed up, with the bandaged puppy, and once the whole story came out asked the cops to drop the charges. So that one ended about the way it should have.

The odd thing about criminal defense is that it isn't about guilt or innocence so much as it is about just exactly how guilty the guy is. The job is a hell of a lot easier if you don't care about either. The two truest things I have ever been told by other wretches flawed enough to make a profession out of defending poor people are quite illuminating. The first one was a friend's response to a non-lawyers common question about how he could stand to defend the obviously guilty.

My friend guffawed and shook his head. "The guilty? Defending the guilty is easy. What scares me is defending the innocent. Too much pressure."

The second one was an unsolicited piece of advice from one of the most fearless, successful, and seemingly gung-ho defenders I have ever known. He told me that the only way to not go crazy in this business is to believe that trials are there for your own personal enjoyment. Screw the client, screw justice, screw all that other hippy jive. So what if you lose? He's the one going to the clink. You get to leave. Oddly enough, he lost it about a decade later but that was more about a divorce than his work. At least I hope so.

The one thing that becomes apparent if you spend enough time doing this kind of work is the general rule that, ironically, the ones that deep down inside just don't give a shit get the better results. To be sure there aren't a whole lot of people running around admitting to not really caring whether their clients wind up in the slammer, so it is trickier than you might think to figure out who really cares. I'm not talking about the guys that don't give a shit about doing a good job as long as they get paid. Those guys are a menace. I mean the guys that want to win for the sake of winning. Hang around enough and sooner or later you figure it out.

The real trick comes when you try to figure out on which side you fall. Not that you want to think about it all that much. There are too many other things to worry about. For example, when you do public defender trial work there are times when you are in an enclosed space with someone whom you would not like to see on TV, much less share a small room with. On my first day as a public defender after fleeing the horrors of big firm corporate practice, I was hanging with the chief attorney when he had a hearing in a murder case. The client was roughly 7 ft tall, and weighed in the neighborhood of 500 pounds. He had "allegedly" killed his mother by hitting her in the head with a sledgehammer, for reasons that were never made clear. The crime scene photos were interesting, even by standards of crime scene photos. She seemed a handsome old woman except for the missing top part of her head. "Allegedly" is in quotation marks as at an earlier hearing the client wailed repeatedly "I don't know why I killt my momma" over and over in a loud voice.

Safe to say the issue of mental competency was in play.

Anyway, I go to the hearing. Afterwards, back at the office the boss asks me to do him a favor. "We need [the client] to sign this release for his medical records. Can you run over to the holding cell and have him sign this? I need to take care of something else."

I think for a second. "So, you want me to go into an

enclosed space with a mammoth sociopath with apparently random violent tendencies, and hand him a pen?"

"Only because a pencil wouldn't be appropriate," he replied. "I will say it would be a bad idea to let him use your back to sign it."

"Quite"

Needless to say, I survived that episode.

A week or so later, I was asked to do another little "favor." We had a client that was willing to plead to first-degree murder, mainly to take advantage of certain quirks in our state constitution and avoid extradition to a different state with the death penalty for a murder there. The plea hearing was the next day, so I agreed to go the 30 miles to the regional jail and go over the documents with the client and prepare him for what would happen at the plea hearing. After I explain to him that he's going to get a life sentence, which he knows, I show him a paper he's required to sign at the hearing. It says that he is aware that if he fails to pay his fines and court costs that the DMV will suspend his driver's license. This is the first time I hear an admitted murderer giggle.

As part of his preparation I inform him he's going to have to tell the judge what he did in order to enter a guilty plea. I suggest he tell me what he plans to say. He says, "Well, I was just lying there with her. I started to strangle her. She stopped struggling but she was still breathing. So I needed something to strangle her with." His eyes seemed to glance down at my tie. (This marked the moment I made a firm policy to never wear a tie in any kind of jail again.) He continued: "So I went out into the other room, took her shoelaces out of her shoes, and finished her off with those."

I said "The judge will ask why you did this."

"I guess it was all that damn crack," he responded. "It sure seemed like a good idea at the time."

Sometimes the struggle isn't with fear, but with shock. I was at the jail some months later conversing with a gentleman accused of sexual molestation. The conversation, as it will when conversing with pedophiles, got a bit weird. I'll skip to the middle.

"I didn't do it," he said. "They is lying. I know those boys and I play with them but I didn't do anything wrong with them."

"How do you play with them?"

"I'd rub and kiss them, maybe lick over their backs. Stuff like that. That's legal, ain't it?"

I kept a complete straight face. "This second charge

says you put your finger in the 6 year old's butt."

"Yeah. I did that too." He then pointed to the first knuckle of his index finger. "I only stuck it in that far. It's not like I fucked him or anything." I shrugged. I then gently described the laws to him, that what he described to me was exactly what he was accused of. He seemed a bit confused and surprised.

So, there is usually something more pressing to worry about than contemplating whether you really give a shit and then trying to figure out how to stop if you do. If you've figured out that your clients are better off if you don't care, and you care about your clients... you can see the problem there. Weird stuff. Better to just go and work in the garden, like that French guy said at the end of that book.

II) Baptism by Nonsense

The Seeks case was the first case I ever took to trial. Dumped in with all the DUI's, bar fights and domestic cases I find an aggravated robbery of a senior citizen. Complaint alleges this dude just broke into his elderly neighbors house, took her purse, dragged her from her bedroom to a staircase and tossed her down the stairs to the basement than ran off.

The preliminary hearing is in a week. A preliminary hearing is a hearing where the state has to show "probable cause" to keep the accused in jail or on bond pending indictment and trial for a felony. By "probable cause" the courts mean "any evidence whatsoever." What really happens is the accused either bargains away the hearing for a lesser bond to get out of jail, or else uses the hearing to "freeze" the testimony of the state's witnesses, that is get what they say on the record so they can't change their stories. Nothing to worry about until then, that is except the million other cases I'm working on.

The day of the preliminary hearing I get word that Seeks has arrived from the regional jail, and that the transport officers have put him in a small room so that I can talk to him in private. Nothing quite like being in a small room with an accused violent felon. I was a rookie back then and I thought maybe these guys were dangerous. Once you get ninety five percent of them sobered up and in jail for a few days then they are just pathetic. Back then I figured maybe he only attacks old people.

I open the door and stroll in. Seeks is sitting at the table, wearing leg chains and handcuffs attached to his waist. Generally this sort of treatment is reserved for the more distinguished violent felons and/or escape risks. From the looks of this guy I have no idea which category he falls into. He's a bit chubby, with a sort of common low-birth face structure. Very southern/rural. Kinky brown hair, a little pale, and he looks a bit worse for the wear for a few days in the clinker.

I sit down and tell him I am his attorney, and ask if he is indeed Thomas Seeks. It wouldn't be the first time a transport officer fucked this up and brought me the wrong guy, and it would be a shame to put some random still half-drunk DUI type through an aggravated robbery prelim. Then again, it might sober him up, but it would waste my time and we know what a tragedy that would be, eh?

He need only say the words "Yessir, I'm Tommy Seeks" for me to cringe a bit. His voice is quite effeminate, which I could care less about but there is this jury issue I have to keep in mind.

So I have a gay-sounding guy, in the rural semi-south, who is accused of breaking into an old lady's house, taking her purse, and throwing her down a staircase. I'm tempted to ask if he raped any children on his way out the door. To my general embarrassment, but to my credit as a pragmatist, the thought "At least he's white" pops into my head.

"So, Tommy, how are they treating you down there?"

He starts crying. I assume this means he isn't happy with the place. "I'm sorry sir. I ain't never hurt nobody. The police just don't like me cause they think I killt someone back a few years and everyone hates me but its all a lie cause people think I'm weird cause I wear capes and smoke a lot of pot. I can't stay in that jail sir. They won't let me smoke there and they keep me in the hole for no reason and see how they have me chained up like this. I didn't rob no old lady, but she's saying I did I bet they told her I killt someone and she's lyin on me. I know who did it but I don't know who he is...."

I thought about interrupting, but the general rule is let 'em go until they stop. Hard enough to get them to talk to go stopping them once they get rolling.

"... cause I don't know his first name he's one of the Frumps but I know his face and know who he knows and maybe you can find him for me. I'm sorry sir... what is your name."

"I'm Elbow Jobertski. I'm your attorney, but I guess you figured that part out already."

"Elbow? That your real name?"

"Yeah. I can't explain it, though."

"Please make it so I don't have to go back to that jail Mr. Elbow. Please do everything you can."

"Sure. First, why don't you cut the crap and give me his first name? At least his street name."

"Billy. I'm sorry, Mr. Elbow. I'm scared to be giving names like that."

IT SAYS HERE...

The time for the hearing was approaching. I needed to go see about a deal for lower bail. "How much bail can you swing Tommy?"

"My dad says they can do twenty thousand if they put up the house."

I check the file. Bail is currently set at fifty thousand. Usually this isn't a problem, but if the local constabulary want a piece of this dude's ass... well... maybe it will be a problem.

So I go looking for George. He's messing with some poor fuckers that can't afford an attorney but don't qualify for a public defender. I get to watch him screw two people into DUIs that even I could beat. The officer isn't even here. Off they go to jail though, guilty or not. I guess when you can admit to driving drunk and get 24 hours or go to trial all by yourself and face a possible six months, well, it can get easy to just admit it whether you did it or not.

I roam around the hall and see an older lady, let's face it, a very old lady showing her bruises to a deputy. She doesn't look very sane: standard issue redneck grandma who has an idea of what moonshine tastes like, weighs less than her age, has odd protrusions from her flesh in unexpected places. She goes on and on to the deputy about

18

her aches and pains. He looks my way with a vacant thousand-yard stare. She then looks my way, catching my eyes. I swear the room gets twenty degrees colder. I go find George. I know what I need to do now.

"Yo George. This Seeks case, how about reducing his bail to ten grand and we forget the prelim?"

"O.K. Let me go talk to the officer."

Normal deal. Now I stand around and try to not look worried. Also try not to look bored, just another day in the life, la la la...

"Good news and bad news. They object to the bail at ten thousand, but they are O.K. with a personal recognizance bond with home confinement."

"Fuuuuuck.. We can't get that down here. We gotta go upstairs to circuit court for that, and we're flipping a coin. Judge Pope will be cool, but if we get Judge Folsom, he's going to bend me over."

George shrugged. "Best I can do. I'll ask for a PR plus home confinement upstairs if you waive the prelim and then move for the bond reduction in Circuit Court. If we have the hearing, well, I don't like hearings..."

"Let me chat with The Doomed."

I slowly return to the room where Seeks is sitting,

chained like some sort of exhibit. I pass a room where I again see the very elderly woman. I gather this is the victim. So I start to parse through the data I have, try to figure out the play. It takes about two seconds, but a little longer to figure out how to explain it to Seeks. He doesn't seem to be a regular in the system, so I may have to be a bit more genteel than I would otherwise.

"Tommy?"

"Yessir?"

"Okay. Here's the deal. The cops won't give you a ten thousand dollar bond, but they will go home confinement and a zero bond. Problem is, we can't get that in magistrate court, so we gotta go to Circuit Court, and while Judge Pope will likely go along, I have a strong feeling Judge Folsom will screw us, cause he likes old people."

"He hates me."

"Well. That cinches it. I still say we go for it, though. The state has the woman here to testify against you, so we will lose the prelim. However, I'm pretty sure Folsom will catch our hearing as Judge Pope is out for the month. So we will get screwed there. Usually I would like to get the lady on the stand, but... ." I paused, and looked hard at Tommy.

"But what?"

"Okay Tommy. This ain't Kindergarten. I'm about to say something that might seem a bit awful and not very nice, but it isn't my job to be nice. It is my job to keep you out of prison. You get that?"

He nodded.

"She's old Tommy, and if she testifies today, and happens to drop dead before the trial, they can try to use that testimony against you. I think we need to just waive the hearing, take our chances with Folsom, and see what happens. Maybe she drops dead, or loses her mind before trial, and then you walk."

"But I didn't do it."

"Yeah, but if today she says you did then she ain't likely going to say different later as she would be looking at a perjury rap. We can't worry about now, you know what the possible sentence is for robbery here? No less than ten years. Our Supreme Court has affirmed sentences of over a hundred years. Judge Folsom loves old people and cops, and the cops hate you, so Folsom might decide to do a tape measure job on your ass."

"Huh?"

"Forget that. I'm just saying he might sentence you to a really big number."

He looked at me. Just pathetic really. "So you are tellin me that I should waive the hearing."

I shrugged. "Yeah Tommy. We have a slight chance of getting you out then, and that way her testimony isn't preserved. I think the prosecutor is making a big mistake here not having her testify. Who knows... maybe Folsom will be in a good mood and grant you your bond."

"Okay sir. I'll trust you."

Then an impromptu Constitutional law class as I explain his rights and where he has to sign to say he doesn't want a preliminary hearing. I let him know that the hearing will likely not be for a few days, as I need to file a motion and schedule a hearing. He wants me to hurry, but I try to make it clear to him that the chance of home confinement is gravy, that we may have saved his ass by not having the hearing. He hears me, but I don't think he is really listening. He's a scared little boy who just wants to go home, and for that I can't blame him.

So I go back to the office, file a boilerplate motion, and schedule a hearing. The Judge's secretary squeezes me in the day after tomorrow. Nice of her.

The day of the hearing, Seeks was led in for his bond hearing, splendidly clad in an orange jumpsuit and handcuffs. Time to joust at a windmill.

"State your appearances for the record" sighed Judge Folsom.

"George Clinton for the State your honor."

"Elbow Jobertski, for the defendant, Thomas Seeks, who is here in person."

"Okay. Why are we here?"

"Your Honor, we are here on a motion for bond redu..."

He cut me off. "I'm aware of that much. Mr. Clinton, what is Mr. Seeks charged with?"

"Robbery, Burglary, Grand Theft, and assault of a person over sixty-five years of age."

"I see. Current bond?"

"Fifty thousand dollars."

"Okay, Mr. Jobertski. What grounds do you have to reduce his bond?"

"Your honor, my client is indigent and cannot possibly raise the bond as set, and as such he is being denied his right to reasonable bail pending trial. The state has agreed to recommend that Mr. Seeks be released on a his own recognizance with the condition of home confinement."

"Where is Mr. Seeks going to stay?"

"His sister's house on the other side of the gorge, north of Grassy Bridge on the Cecil County border. "

"Where does his victim live?"

"The alleged victim lives roughly thirty miles away on the other side of the gorge in southern Elm Meadow."

"Mr. Clinton, how old is this victim?"

"A seventy-two year old woman, Your Honor."

"What exactly did Mr. Seeks do to her ?"

"Threw her down a flight of stairs."

"I see." Folsom shuffled through some papers. "Mr. Seeks, I've decided to give you half of what you want. The order of this court is that defendant's motion is granted as to the part requesting home confinement. However, given the severity of the crime, I deny the motion for reduction of bond, and this Court on its own motion orders that Mr. Seeks' bond be increased to one hundred fifty thousand dollars, cash only. Anything further, counsel?"

"No sir," Mr. Clinton and I said nearly in unison.

"Then court is adjourned. Mr Seeks is placed in the custody of the Sheriff's department pending trial."

"Thank you, your honor," I said in a clear, loud voice, as is the quaint custom when a judge screws you over.

The bailiff led Seeks off through some passage over to the holding cells to wait for transport to the jail.

So I go back to the office. I've nothing better to do.

Nothing much happens in these cases until an indictment comes down from the grand jury. The client sits in jail and loses his shit, calls once a week and writes letters. Seeks didn't have much to do but sit around the jail thinking, and he wasn't good at that. He convinced himself it was a good idea to write a letter to the prosecutor, who, being a decent sort, sent it to me unopened. I had to have a little chat with my boy after that.

Going to the regional jail is a pain. It's about a thirty minute drive. Once there, you have to fill out some forms, have your bags looked through. Pens are fine. Under no circumstances can you take your keys. I think I'd be able talk them into letting me have a gun before I'd get my keys through. They'd let me hang them from a rung in a closet by the sally port because they liked me. Asshole attorneys either had to leave them in a car or take their chances with the "lockers" in the general visiting area.

So I get through the port, and sit in one of the interview rooms. It has a table and a bunch of porch furniture type chairs, florescent lighting, and that hard-to-describe smell of the jail. Best one-word description is "stale." These rooms have no ventilation once the door is shut, which makes the smell collect and intensify. Usually I stand in the doorway until the client arrives, both for the comparatively fresh air and to make sure the guards don't forget I'm there.

Finally they lead Seeks down the hall to me. I motion to a chair, he sits, I sit across from him and throw the letter on the table.

"Are you fucking stupid?" No point in being half-assed about it. He was pressed for a reply. "I told you not to talk to anyone about your case. No one. I told you if a cop or anyone tried to get you to talk about it to just keep asking for a lawyer. So, is it my fault for not specifically telling you to not write a letter to the fucking prosecutor?"

"I'm sorry. It just seemed like a good idea for some reason."

"Listen. It's hard here. I get that. You have nothing to do but stir and think and you are going to have all sorts of dumb ideas. Here is what you do. Write whoever the fuck you want about whatever you want. Write the judge. Write God. Write to Stevie Nicks (I'd learned by that point that he was somehow a huge Stevie Nicks fan). Just one thing. Now you listinin' to me?

"Yessir."

"When you put the letter in the envelope, you better damn well be addressing it to me. You got that? You don't need to fuck this up and do fifty years. Send it to me. Got it?

"Yessir."

"Alright. Now you want to talk to me about this whole murder bullshit?"

I'd been over his version of the robbery case. Simple enough. He was in his house, drinking and smoking pot with who must have been Billy Frump. I could account for his other brothers as they were in jail that night after a bar fight. Billy Frump got up and left. A few minutes later, Frump banged on his back window. Seeks opened the window and Frump handed him a purse. Seeks made him take the purse back and slammed the window shut and went to sleep. Three hours later the police were banging on the front door. Seeks' front door was locked from the inside with a padlock for which he has no key; Seeks would go in and out through the window. This startled the cops who grabbed him and roughed him up a bit. He was taken to jail. That was pretty much it.

I couldn't find Frump. He was part of a family of criminal all-stars. Claude, Joe Bob, and Maurice were around. Just no Billy. His brothers said he hadn't been around in about a year, but I don't think they thought I'd believe that. However, I kept hearing something about a murder. Seeks would mention it but he didn't want to say anything. His letter mentioned the murder. I wanted to know what the fuck was going on.

"You know that Bobby Dunkel kid that got killed about three years ago?"

"I'd never heard of this place three years ago," I replied.

"I's at my house. Not this one but the one I lived in before. We would always be partying there. Drinking and stuff. We had a big place to have fires and we were right by the woods so we'd have big bonfires and people'd always be hanging around there partying. I went to sleep one time and in the morning I got up, well, like three PM and the pit was full like they'd been burning all kinds of wood in there. Nobody came around that night. The next day I was going

28

to build another fire so I got some of the old wood we got and when I got to the pit I figured I'd best clean out some of the ashes and spent wood. I get a shovel and a barrow and I make a trip and then I come back and another and on maybe the third load when I brought up the shovel I'd liked to have a heart attack 'cause there was what looked like a human skull. I figured someone been funnin' me 'till I found more bones. I ran to the neighbors screaming telling them to call the law someone been kilt.

Them cops come and they went through all the bones and all the stuff and took it all away. That's all I know for sure. I know that Dunkel kid disappeared about that time but they couldn't ever do one of them D and A tests so they really don't know. None of the people at that party say they saw nothin. Won't say a word. They thought Jeff Wilkins done it for a while, but Sammy Dunkell who is Bobby's daddy kilt him but then someone tell the cops Jeff was out of town. Everyone thinks I did it. That's why the cops hate me. I didn't rob no old lady but I tellin you the cops tell her to lie on me anyway. She don't know who did it, they tellin her it me so they can lock me up They ain't got no witnesses or evidence I done no murder so they arrest me for anything else they can."

"Who is this 'we' you were partying with?"

"A bunch of people. Bobby Dunkel, Janie Smith, Mary Crawford, Billy Tyler, Chicago Joe, Mohawk, Crawdad, Lil' bit..."

"I get the idea." He was naming the Catlett Creek crowd, a bunch of people that lived up Catlett hollow over in south Elm Hill. It wasn't the money side of town and most of that group had frequent flier cards at the public defender office. Fun people to hang out with, if you knew how to properly use a ketchup bottle as a weapon. They also had pretty spotty memories when it came to anything a lawyer or cop wanted to know unless it helped them. No help there.

"Not much we can do for the next while," I said. We have an idea of what they say you did, and I have your story. It's hard as hell to figure out how to prove nothing happened. They have to indict you in the next three months or they have to let you go. I'm guessing they will indict you. What that means is the officer goes before a grand jury, a bunch of randomly selected people, and shows them the evidence. Then the grand jury votes on whether to indict you. If that happens we go back to court to get a trial date, and then I get all their evidence so we can maybe work out something."

Seeks sighed. "I don't know how much longer I can stand this place, Mr. Elbow."

"I hear you. Just remember to address those letters to me. You hearin' me?"

"Yessir."

Over the next month and a half nothing really happened in Seeks' case. There were other cases, other clients to worry about. I'd deal with officers that handled Seeks' case; one in particular was a good sort, and a bright fellow. His only flaw is that he wasn't as bright as he thought he was, and when someone's carrying a badge that makes him a bit dangerous. He was a great uniformed officer. Smart, fair, useful. Then they made him a detective, and unfortunately he figured the promotion made him a genius. He started dressing like he figured a detective should, which for him was something like a combination of Tom Landry and Sherlock Holmes. He actually carried around a pipe for a while and I still don't know where he found those hats. Great hats.

I couldn't really fault him. He should have been proud. It didn't occur to me that his style had a lot to do with the fact that he was almost certainly the first person in his family to ever wear a suit to work. He gave up the pipe after a few months, and was going to give up the hats, but I talked him back into the hats. They really worked for him. Very film noir.

During these months he did something I thought was really stupid, but years later I wondered if it wasn't subtle genius. I was trying a marijuana case. Some kid gets caught with a little too much weed in more than one bag, and gets charged with possession with intent to deliver, a felony. The usual defense, if the evidence isn't suppressed for an illegal search or whatnot, is personal use, which makes it a misdemeanor. Juries there didn't care to convict for small amounts of pot, even if the kid was a black kid going to Gauley State down in the valley. Which is saying something. So for the most part I would be trying to make light of the fact we were wasting all this time on a pot case.

Well, this Detective, The Hat, was the arresting officer. Said he got a tip about some other illegal activity, someone stealing a four-wheeler or something, and he knocked on the door of the house to talk to my client. My client opens the door, and The Hat said he "detected an odor that based on his training and experience as a police officer he identified as marijuana." The Hat then asks if there are any drugs in the residence, and my client admits he's been smoking weed. My client gives The Hat consent to search, and The Hat finds three small baggies and about $300 in smallish bills.

All fine and good, except for some reason he went sideways during his testimony. George was the prosecutor. When he asked the officer how he could identify the odor, The Hat gave the pat response about academy training. For some reason he also added that he remembered smelling it in his fraternity house back when he was down at State. Which opened the door for me to give him ten different kinds of shit on cross-examination about his college days and how often there was smoke, did he see the bags, why would such a sterling officer such as himself and so on.

The whole point was to hopefully underline how silly it is to try to put a guy in prison for something so common that the arresting officer was casually around it back when. Combine that with my patented "potato chip defense," and we were home free. The potato chip defense would be me getting up at closing, walking over towards the center of the jury box and saying something like: "Ladies and Gentlemen of the Jury. The state would have you believe that because some kid has a few bags of something that means he's sellin' it. This makes no sense."

I'd pause and walk over towards the state's table a bit. "I like potato chips. Sometimes I just have to have potato chips. So I go down to the corner store, but all they have are those silly little bags that have like five chips in them. So I wind up buying five or six of the little things so I can have a decent amount of chips. Don't mean I'm sellin' em."

Then I'd pace back over to the side of the box closer to the bench. Making eye contact here or there. Draw 'em in. "My wife. She likes chips too. She's not like me though. She don't want to have too many chips at once. So she'll go to the store and buy one of those big bags with all those little bags in them. Then she'll just take out one bag and eat those. She not planning on selling them."

Then back to the center. "Look. There's all kinds of reasons someone would want smaller bags. The laws are easier if you aren't carrying that much at once. Sure, the state says he has all that cash. That don't mean he's a dealer. Lots of people who live 'round there work under the table and stuff. Lots of people don't have bank accounts. He had the pot. He was smoking it. He admitted it then and I'm telling you now. But if having three bags of something means you are meaning to sell it, I hope I don't get stopped on the way back from the store and get in trouble for not having a business license..."

I'd go on a bit about reasonable doubt. George would get up and respond how he could, and the jury would go out and come back ten minutes later with the misdemeanor. If I tried this with cocaine, they'd come back with a felony. So it isn't like I'm Gerry Spence or anything.

The word spread around lawyer circles pretty quickly about The Hat's nostalgic testimony about his college years, and within a week every defense lawyer in town had a copy of the transcript. What this meant was The Hat was out of the narcotics business, which probably put his job at risk except that he was doing a good job so they let him just do other crimes. Which was probably exactly what he wanted. He just wasn't the type to want to bust people for silly shit. If there was any big traffic going on the Feds took over the investigation anyway.

So they'd also assign the unusual cases to him to make up for the drug cases he couldn't do. The most memorable was the computer fraud case. You just don't see a whole lot of felony computer fraud in rural public defender work, especially back then. Back when internet auction sites were sort of a new thing The Hat apparently got some sort of notice that there was a kid in the county selling items and those items just not reaching the buyers. So I wind up with a computer fraud file. The prelim didn't last very long after I asked The Hat about IP addresses. He looked at me confused and the magistrate asked me what I was talking about. I glanced sideways at the prosecutor, he stood up and asked for a recess and then offered a misdemeanor and a five dollar fine.

The kid took it, mainly because he was guilty as hell and who knows whether or not a jury and a rural Judge would grasp the internet or if it would matter and fuck it. Get out clean.

Eventually, they indicted Seeks. In larger counties the prosecutor will convene several grand juries during a term and each judge would have three or so sets of arraignment hearings with maybe six or seven people. In a more rural county, the grand jury meets once per term, every four months. This county was big enough for two judges, and they would each wind up with about twenty-five indictments. An indictment is when the grand jury decides to formally accuse someone of a crime, and an arraignment is when the accused is officially notified of the indictment, enters a plea and given a trial date. Usually the formal reading is waived. I was always tempted to ask for it in one of those two hundred count molestation cases, but figured given the power of consecutive sentencing the client needed as much goodwill with the judge as possible.

The old style courtrooms look a bit like a church. The gallery behind the counsel tables was made up of wooden pews like in a church. In more modern courtrooms you see maybe five or six rows. In this one there were twenty. A throwback to times when communities would actually show up to watch most trials. The place was always empty except on arraignment days. For each session there would be twenty five defendants, almost all with direct and even extended family present. Some, like Seeks, would still be in jail. It looked a lot like Sunday morning at a local church, except fewer snakes.

Yeah, snakes. We had a lot of that going on. I had a wild battery case where some woman drove up from Alabama for the sole purpose of beating the shit out of another woman. Turned out the second woman, an attractive woman in her early twenties, somehow coaxed the rich fifty-five year old father of the first woman up to Franklin County and married him. Then she started making him go to church, and as I understood it, refused to fuck him until he "proved his faith in God to her." This of course involved handling the snakes, mainly timber-rattlers.

I guess the poor guy really was hard up and he went along with it. He didn't know what he was doing and wound up over at Franklin General Hospital full of anti-venom and clinging to life. Meanwhile there was this will naming his new wife the sole heir. Ergo, the can of whup-ass.

These arraignment hearings are more or less a ceremonial activity. It would always crack me up when I'd open the paper and see a headline on the order of "Joe Blow Denies Allegations" and then see that the whole thing was based on a "not guilty" plea at arraignment. You always plead not guilty. If you don't, the judge will enter it. Constitutional niceties make pleading guilty a time consuming exercise where the defendant has to be instructed as to every right being waived, the judge has to be satisfied that the guy is sober, sane, not being forced, and believes his attorney isn't a walking piece of shit. That also cracks me up, in one of those hearings when the judge will ask the defendant if he was satisfied with my representation. He doesn't care, he just needs it on the record in case the guy comes back at some point and accuses me of being a dipshit.

However, the judge does have to find that "the defendant is represented by an attorney competent in criminal matters." Which is often the nicest thing I hear said about me in a given week.

Anyway, you always plead not guilty. I've actually had to argue with clients about it, something like the following:

"You also are going to be asked to enter a plea. Tell the judge "Not Guilty.""

"But I'm guilty."

"That's just dandy. Lets just keep that between you and me for now. Pleading guilty is complicated and we are going to want to negotiate what exactly you are pleading guilty to. Right now just plead 'Not Guilty.'"

"I don't want to lie..."

"Listen," I'd sigh. "This isn't a factual question we are dealing with. Whether you are actually guilty doesn't matter. All they are asking is whether or not you want to have a trial. You aren't guilty unless either the state proves you are or if you tell them you are. It is always 'not guilty.' The last time someone insisted on pleading guilty the Judge entered a 'not guilty' plea anyway. Right now you are not guilty. This is a fact. You are not guilty."

"But I don't want a trial."

"Yes you do. Right now, you want a trial. Hell, you just think you might have done something. For all you know it isn't the crime they are charging. If it turns out they have you, then we can enter a plea later. Right now, doing anything but saying 'not guilty' would be really stupid. You aren't lying."

"Okay, I guess."

Seeks wasn't difficult about this, seeing he didn't think he was guilty and all.

I'd have about eight clients in each session. People would murmur around, I'd find the ones out on bond and explain what was going on and such. The sign that the festivities were about to start was when the bailiffs would lead those still in jail into the courtroom and into their reserved front row. The Chief Public Defender would be sitting at the defense table with a bunch of affidavits filed by people without attorneys and who wanted one assigned. The other public defender and I would be hanging out behind the jury box with other members of the bar, some of who had clients, others who were looking to pick up an appointment. If there was a person who qualified for a lawyer and for some reason the Public Defender office couldn't take the case, like a conflict, it would be assigned to a private attorney who could bill the state for not so much but better than nothing per hour. The judge was supposed to go off a list, but he'd just pick whoever was there and willing.

There were three attorneys in the Public Defender office. A Chief Public Defender and two "Assistant Public Defenders." I was an assistant. The Chief was an older grizzled functional alcoholic who had bounced around for a while, spent some time as a prosecutor in Georgia, and wound up having his resume picked out of a pile when they opened the office back in the mid-80's when most of the local bar got tired of being forced to do criminal cases for a crappy rate.

The Chief was the kind of attorney that would drive serious students of the practice of criminal defense completely insane. The Chief was amicable and casual about things, and didn't exactly burn up the office getting ready for a trial. While most lawyers would be running around researching this and getting a color diagram for that and pestering this witness about the other thing, The Chief would have went to the bar or whatnot and chatted with the main officer to see what he'd say and what the witnesses would say. He knew that the prosecutor probably told the witnesses to not talk to him, anyway.

Then The Chief would retire to the office with a twelve-pack and a bottle of bourbon. He'd review the police file and then just sit in the dark and think about the case, drinking cold beer and taking the occasional jolt of bourbon. The next day, he'd be ready for battle.

He wouldn't come out with a huge fancy defense. He'd just sit there. He'd get up and ask two or three questions that didn't seem a big deal. Then on closing argument those three answers by an officer or witness would let him completely take the wheels off of the state's case and drive it into a ditch. It was supernatural. The prosecutors tended to be terrified of him. It wasn't like he won every case, but he would maybe two times out of ten win a case that was by all rights completely not winnable. The prosecutor knew better than to try a weak case against him, those would result in guilty pleas to far lesser charges. Battle was joined only when the prosecutor had what looked like a water-tight case and couldn't offer a deal the defendant would take.

One time he did it not only by not asking questions, but by specifically refusing to object. He's just sitting there, and the prosecutor is trying to sneak some obvious hearsay statement in about something or other. It was in front of Judge Folsom, who was the sort of serious type that The Chief drove crazy. Folsom interrupted the witness and asked The Chief if he was going to object.

"Noooooooo Your Honor, We have nooooothing to hide," replied The Chief, raising his hands out to his sides in a gesture of openness.

This of course, caused the jury to pay really close attention to the answer, and that was the answer that The Chief used to plant the seed of doubt. He had a knack of seeing a case from the outside and figuring out where he could attack with the least amount of fuss. He told me several times that a jury just doesn't trust a really active and intense defense attorney unless an argument for actual innocence could be made. In cases where you have to pick and sew doubt, you have to be as much of an underdog as you can. Otherwise the jury will think it is picking between your story and the state's, and then you are dead. It is very important in bad cases to do everything to make sure the jury knows you aren't there to sell them anything, that you are there to explain why they shouldn't buy what the state is selling.

Besides The Chief and myself there was one other lawyer in the office. He's a lifelong native of Franklin County, knows where the bodies are buried, an odd fellow with a mild drinking problem, the type where he disappears for a day or two and then stumbles in the office in bad shape and says he really just felt the need to sit in the dark drinking bourbon and listening to Gordon Lightfoot records. For no adequately explained reason he called me "Stud Duck." I tended to call him by the cleverly created sobriquet "Bill." We get along alright, despite the fact I'm in his eyes somewhat of a "dammyankee" as I grew up in that little bit of West Virginia that is north of the Mason-Dixon line.

Hanging out with Bill has its hazards. I did allow him to "show me around the county" during my first few weeks there. This amounted to going to every dive bar in the county where "I might have to look for a witness someday." I figured that if I kept coming back to those places it would be more likely I'd be a witness. The kind of place where half the people are worried about spilling their beer on the half that deep down inside want beer to be spilled on them. You see the odd flannel shirt and rebel flag, and maybe hear some country music.

Mainly I just tried to not spill my beer on anyone.

I also saw the sights. The crappy little place where Hank Williams was last seen alive. Had a beer. Some bar owned by some guy who played linebacker for St. Louis back in the '70s. Had a beer there too. Pretty much had a beer in every disreputable bar in the county, which is damn close to all of them. All of this by seven in the afternoon on a weekday. By then we went to the one "reputable" joint, where all the lawyers hung out.

Which bars are reputable is a matter of perspective, it seems to me these days...

Right. But then there were the public defender conferences. A weekend where all the defenders in the state converged on some innocent state park resort type thing to drink, grill, and maybe accidentally wander into a presentation. Generally I'd stumble upon enough legal education credits in these things to have way more than I needed to keep my license. The problem is that someone who had apparently never read Aristotle decided that all us lawyers would cut out the double-billing, the laziness, and the simple theft of client money if we watched enough presentations telling us about ethics.

So we needed three hours in ethics every two years. The yearly conference featured a nice hour and a half presentation. Usually last to sorta blackmail us into seeing other things. So this one time Bill and I both need the ethics hours, so we go catch a whole afternoon. Fine. The first guy was pretty typical. A blood spatter expert. Like usual he's a retired cop, like usual he hits the high notes in the first thirty minutes and then drives us nuts with useless details for a while. Then he, as is the usual custom, suggests that "you kinds of lawyers" try to "distort the truth." Then in turn the "True Believer" types get their backs up, and then it really gets ugly...

Pretty standard.

What was not pretty standard was the next one about finding signs of child abuse. It started with the pattern. Some useful information. Pictures of children burned with steam irons. All claim the child was playing and pulled it down on them, but the expert showed the signs to look for that indicate accident versus deliberate injury. The woman was a doctor at some big pediatric hospital. Italian name, but she was most definitely Indian. University of Bombay or something. Maybe this cultural difference explains some of the following, but her accented English really played a part in the absurdity that was about to play out.

She segued into sexual abuse. Well, really didn't segue. She had one of those powerpoint type deals, using a clicker and a laser pointer. She popped right up there a picture of a rather gynecological view of some small girls primary sex organ. Out of nowhere, really. Fine. She pointed out some detail. I figured that would be it.

Wrong.

Way Wrong.

Then a second picture. Some damage there. The third, and this is one of the things I can't figure out, was animated with some sort of close/open action. Every picture seemed to be the last one. Then there was another. For a while it was tears and such. Then the hymen. A big picture of every kind of hymen, one after the other. Probably twenty in all. Just huge vaginas being described in this Indian-accented English that sorta made the whole scene perfect.

I was in the back, mainly watching people try not to watch the screen. She would ask whether "we wanted to see more of this type." The group would quickly indicate the negative, and a sense of relaxation would sweep the room...

Then the lady would show another type of hymen. By "no more of this type" she meant that particular version of a child's vagina. Not vaginas in general. Not even Eve Ensler ever got this far out of control.

Why bring this up when speaking about Bill? Well, at about picture eighteen Bill leaned over and whispered into my ear. What he whispered threw me into one of those fits of trying-like-hell-not-to-laugh-at-a-really-socially-awkward-time. I wound up sweating, hands in face, upper body shaking, and so on. Brutal. What he whispered was this:

"I think that last one was my granddaughter."

I made it to the end. Almost. At some point the lady said "This is all of the vagina pictures." The room swayed with relief.

Then she put up a big picture of an anus.

I did survive, much more experienced for the next time. Helpful hint: When sitting next to someone in a really uncomfortable situation like that, always be the first to make the sick joke. Take the offensive.

Bill hated to go to trial. He was always paranoid

about losing his license for really odd reasons, like arguing to a jury that they should find his client not guilty when his client actually was guilty. Which is weird seeing you can lose your license for not doing it. What you are doing is arguing that the state's evidence allows for a reasonable conclusion that doesn't involve guilt. He had it mixed up in his head with the idea that we weren't allowed to present false evidence, which is a totally different deal.

So Bill had some interesting ways of avoiding trial. He had an extremely effective method for getting people who didn't want to plead guilty to a misdemeanor to plead guilty rather than taking their chance at trial. A misdemeanor is a minor offense, a felony is the more serious variety. Back a few hundred years ago all felonies were punishable by death. Now, a felony is punishable by more than a year in prison, and a misdemeanor by up to a year in jail. Jails and prisons are two very different thing. Jails are run by a county or city, here the cities and counties pool resources to have a regional jail. A prison is run by the state. There are obvious differences in clientele, seeing one is full of felons and one of guys awaiting trial, serving misdemeanor sentences, and those waiting to be transferred to a prison after being sentenced.

IT SAYS HERE...

What Bill would do to get a client to plead to a misdemeanor instead of risking a felony is put a penny and a half-dollar on the desk in front of the client. "Look here," he'd say, pointing at the penny. "This is your asshole after jail." He'd point at the half-dollar. "This is your asshole after prison."

This worked quite well, as you probably could imagine.

Seeks got through the arraignment quite smoothly, and was led back to jail. We were given a trial date on a Monday five weeks away. Actually, all of my cases were given that same trial date. Usually most of these would plead out, and if not these cases would be tried one after the other that week. Usually a "speedy trial" was when a person was tried as soon as possible after his arrest. Folsom took it to a new level. His trials rarely stretched into a second day.

Now that Seeks had been arraigned, I had access to the discovery. I really couldn't count on all that much assistance from The Chief or Bill unless I was looking for some sort of zen or if I wanted to go tour bars again. No big deal. If I lose the case he probably spends the rest of his life in prison. So I'd have to figure all this out for myself.

Until now, I had access only to the initial police report. Now I have a lot of The Hat's investigation. The exact statement made by the woman, for one thing, on tape:

"I's goin to bed that night and I knew somethin' was not right so I left the light on. I's havin' trouble sleepin' 'cause of my nerves were bad. I just knew somethin' was wrong. Then 'round midnight sure 'nuff I see this black thing at the foot of my bed. I a' asked who it was and it said 'Tommy Seeks.' He told me to get out of bed and show him where my money was at. He grabbed me and drug me out the room and 'cross the kitchen and threw me down the stairs. By the time I's able to get back up to call the law he'd done hit the alarm thing and busted through my front door. I looked all over but I ain't seen my purse since. I knew that Seeks was trouble. Something not right with that boy."

Which was odd. When I saw the woman in the courtroom she wore glasses. I made a note to see if I could figure out just how blind she was without them. Need to do it quietly as not to tip off anyone and trigger her sudden memory about how she had time to put on her glasses or some such. Plus this business of the guy telling her who he was was a bit weird.

IT SAYS HERE...

The Hat's report was interesting. Fingerprints from the alarm system came back inconclusive. This is normal. The only case I personally know of where fingerprints were found and identified was one a number of years later when I was doing appellate work. The prosecutor in that case went as far as to exclaim to the judge in a hearing of some sort that "We even have fingerprint evidence! We never have that!" There was a mention of tool mark analysis on the cellar door, which was the obvious point of entry. However, the officers never found anything that could have been used to pry the door open, so that fizzled.

More interesting was his finding a single set of footprints through the dew on the grass, footprints leading to the back of Seeks' house. Just one set. Didn't mention searching for footprints leading away from the house though.

The report mentioned that they got a warrant to search Seeks' house. They found a rusted padlock on the door leading in. When they pounded on the door Seeks climbed out the window, apparently a bit groggy from sleep. There was nothing about his being roughed up, big surprise there. When asked, he told the officers that he didn't have a key for the lock, so he went in and out of the front window. The officers entered the house, and noted that there was a plastic wading pool in the kitchen. What they didn't find was the purse. I also noted that they didn't find a pair of shoes with grass on them. They arrested Seeks, and he's been in jail since. He clammed up when he heard the charges, as he'd been through the system before and he didn't want to talk about the purse. He knew they wanted him no matter what he said.

So, the evidence sucked. Fit right with my client's story, that all he knew about it was Billy Frump waking him up and trying to give him a purse. No purse, just a curious and unlikely identification. No other physical evidence. Nothing.

This was just from the discovery a very winnable case. Stakes were high, though. Robbery including force carried a sentence from anywhere between ten years and infinity. There wasn't a maximum. The wisdom among the bar was that Folsom would give him sixty years for that. In real terms that would be fifteen years before he was parole eligible, and if he behaved himself he'd get one day of good time for every day he served, which gets him out in thirty years. There was also a burglary charge. That carried a determinate one to fifteen year sentence, meaning that he would be eligible for parole after one year, and with good time max out at seven and a half. So if the judge ran this all consecutive he would face at least sixteen years, possibly seventy-five years, but probably no more than thirty-seven and a half.

A bit big for a first trial, I thought. Later I figured that the whole thing was a setup. It was a weak case, but The Powers That Be wanted Seeks taken out of circulation. So they pressured The Chief to dump it on the new guy. The Chief had to answer to a board made up of three local attorneys and two local non-attorneys, and the poor guy was a functional alcoholic and a bit of a problem gambler. He wouldn't be able to make as much anywhere else as he did there, considering benefits. So the board had him by the short hairs.

We didn't have investigators on staff; we had a few we could hire in really big cases, but this, as it turns out, wasn't quite in that league. So I had to do my own snooping. Fun.

The two obvious things I had to look into were Billy Frump and the eyesight of the old lady. Frump was just a matter of asking around. If I found him easily, he wouldn't be much use because that means he wasn't hiding. If he was hard to find, well, you see the problem. Hopefully I'd just run into him, one of his brothers, or at least one of his crowd. He was another one of those Catlett Creek people. If I could manage to figure something out without having to go down into that particular hollow, so much the better. Odds are someone from there would wind up getting arrested for something; maybe I could bump into someone at the courthouse. Plus I could check the court records, see if he had anything pending or was on probation or something.

I had no clue how to get into the eyesight question. I figured I'd just go around the neighborhood where she lived and ask around. Buddy up to a relative or neighbor and ask the odd friendly question. I'd have to take a good look at the crime scene, anyway.

That afternoon I went over to the area where all this happened. Small area around an old company store, a building that is rather more impressive than what the word "store" would conjure up among normal people. Back in the day if you worked in a mine and lived in the company town the company owned your ass. Paid you in company money that could only be used in the company store. So it was usually a decent sized deal, seeing it was the only place miners could buy food, clothing, furniture, and also mining equipment as the miners had to pay for that themselves. Plus the coal companies would put all their local offices in there, so it was a large well-built structure surrounded by the small shacks that the miners rented from that same company.

The company town system was gone, along with most of the mining jobs. However the people remained since they really had nowhere else to go. The store was closed, or at least had moved a few miles up the road and renamed itself "Wal-Mart."

The houses were identical. Tiny one-floor living area with a basement. The basement was for the miner to enter the house after work and clean himself off before coming upstairs as not to make a huge mess. This is why in your serious blue-collar areas you always see a shower in the basement. Just a little tip for you that has nothing to do with the story.

I went and looked around Seeks' place. Nobody was living there. The lock was still on the door. The window didn't open. I could see the wading pool in the kitchen. No real help there. While standing on the porch I saw a station wagon pull up in front of the next house over, the one I figured was the old lady's. A woman seemed to be unloading groceries. Maybe time to go be neighborly.

Approaching strangers can be tricky, and I'm sure investigators have a bunch of theories and methods to do this sort of thing. I wouldn't know, seeing as I'm not an investigator. I just go up to people and start talking. Sometimes I'm surprised as to what comes out of my mouth. Usually it works.

"Hello. Are you related to Ms. Cafferty?" Direct approach.

"She's my mother in law," replied the woman. Neat thing about rural areas. People will talk to you for at least a few minutes before the "Who the fuck are you and what the fuck do you want?" reflex kicks in. In a bigger city on the east coast this takes about three seconds. "She moved out after her attack and we've been staying here until she can sell it."

"She was attacked?"

"Probably not. The old lady's crazy. She's always screaming about people out to get her and so on."

"Does she by any chance wear glasses?" I meant to make up some bullshit about me looking after my friend's house, but rural politeness being what it is I couldn't even get that far.

"Jesus. She's blind without them. The crazy bitch will call our house about once every two weeks because she knocked them off of the table or whatever and is afraid she will step on them. My husband winds up having to go over there before work and help her."

That is about where the reflex kicked in, I could see the spark in her eyes. So I suddenly had to be going nice to meet her and so on, and I had to go talk to a few more people about their insurance and I walked down the street, figuring I'd just knock on a door. Doing that is risky, not so much because you might get shot or hurt as much as you might have someone invite you in for some coffee or a beer and well, you will just wish they shot you after that.

Thankfully the first door I knocked on revealed an older lady that wasn't about to invite me in but was thrilled to have someone to complain about that crazy retard (I'm guessing Seeks) and the batty old lady and how thrilled she was when they both got flushed out of the neighborhood. Nothing helpful, but kept me out of trouble long enough for the daughter-in-law to go inside so I could get back to my car without too much bother. I'd found out what I needed about the old lady, or as much as I was going to find without some kind of medical record subpoena that never occurred to me at the time. That and Folsom would have told me to shove it up my ass. Plus it would have just alerted the prosecution to a possibly devastating cross examination. Once they realized I knew she was blind she would have been sleeping while wearing her glasses since birth. Call it a hunch.

After that I mostly went to court and looked after my other cases. Once in a while I would try to "prepare" for the trial and then realize that I had no solid idea of how. Law School mostly deals with civil cases, and civil cases allow a whole shitload more discovery than a criminal case. In a civil case I could "depose" all the other side's witnesses. This means I could get them in a room with a court reporter, and make them under oath answer any question I cared to ask. Which means I'd have an idea of what they would say. In a criminal case I could ask witnesses to talk to me. Funny thing there, witnesses would seem to think they shouldn't. I'd hate to accuse any prosecutor of out-and-out saying or even trying to put into the head of a witness that she shouldn't talk to the defense attorneys or investigators or whatever.

I'd hate to because there is usually never any solid

proof. Even when a witness claimed she was told not to talk to us, that little "misunderstanding" would be "cleared up" by the time trial or a motion on prosecutorial misconduct rolled around. Then the Judge would promptly rule that he could give a shit.

So they fucking well did it, but good luck doing anything about it. As far as state witnesses the state would turn over any statements if there were any, and experts would have to turn over a bunch of stuff. After that, break out the crystal ball or start believing in remote-viewing or some bullshit. The best you can do is make educated guesses based on experience and the little hard evidence you can find. Good thing I had all that experience drawn from Law School and spending a year writing letters to insurance companies about every little detail and legal issue in some case about bent steel beams. So I had that going for me.

I knew the old bat was blind. On the other hand, Billy Frump wasn't exactly easy for me to see. I ran into one of his brothers, Maurice, who claimed Billy moved to Kentucky about a year and a half ago. I wouldn't have believed that even if I didn't already know he had been arrested for a public intoxication a week before the whole

Seeks robbery mess happened. The magistrate took a guilty plea at the arraignment and fined him ten bucks, and that was the end of it.

It wasn't like I could draw a bunch of Watergate type conclusions and suspicions from Maurice Frump's lie. Lying to cops, or anyone wearing a tie was pretty much a reflex for someone who grew up in Catlett Creek. He didn't brush me off, we had a decent conversation about the weather and WVU football before I asked about his brother, he didn't change tone, didn't suddenly look surprised or guarded. He just answered in stride. Smooth. So I didn't take a whole bunch from that except that while Billy wasn't in Kentucky, he was for damn sure not in Franklin County for what could be a million reasons, but making sure nobody asked him about Seeks' claims could be one.

I was trying, but Jim Rockford I wasn't. I was pretty much stuck there. Even if Billy happened to be around the word that Seeks's lawyer was looking for him would be enough to get him to dust off his copy of "West of the Mississippi on Two Felonies a Week" and take his profession on the road. So I went to plan B, which was to worry and review what I had over and over and hope that somewhere in all of this was something helpful that I missed the first fifty times I reviewed it.

So I wrote out an opening statement. Practiced it a few times. Wrote down all the information each state witness was probably going to say, and tried to imagine objections that could come up. Played a lot of golf with a squirrel dancing in my stomach. The trial drew closer, and I just had to accept the only thing I couldn't do was be more experienced. I didn't have to like it or feel comfortable about it though.

The morning of trial, the nerves were still in control. I did manage to sleep, but I got up really early and went to the office. I sat in there staring at the files, thinking about my opening statement, hoping I came across with some confidence. That would be easy if I at least had some confidence. Or even some experience.

It all came down to the old lady and how she would react to the whole glasses issue. I'd decided not to call any experts about the vision thing, I figured she'd be wearing glasses; my information was somewhat clear that she never wore contacts. I had that. I had the lack of forensic evidence, the lack of shoes with grass on them, and the rest.

They had a poor old lady who was going to say my client, a person she knew, dragged her across the floor and tossed her down a flight of stairs. This was trouble. I went to the courthouse about an hour early, to get situated and so on.

George wandered into the courtroom about ten minutes after me. He was notorious for being skittish on trial day. Until that point, the deal was a plea to a first degree robbery, with a binding twenty years. This wasn't bad, seeing the smart money was on Seeks being convicted and getting sixty years on the robbery, plus the one to fifteen on the burglary. This would be sixteen years to parole eligibility and thirty seven and a half hears maximum assuming he earned all of his "good time" credits. The twenty year sentence would be five years to parole eligibility, ten to kill.

This morning he offered ten years. Two and a half to the board, five to kill. On paper a great deal. It was on Seeks. I hated to advise someone who claims he wasn't guilty to take a plea, but the difference between at least sixteen years and two and a half is quite a bit. Quite a bit more all in all than I judged our chances at trial.

The transport officer brought Seeks in about twenty minutes before kickoff. I told him about the deal.

"I ain't pleadin' guilty, I didn't do it. I just can't.

"I understand. I just want to make sure you consider this. It could be huge. Folsom could put you away for good if we lose this thing."

"We ain't gonna lose this thing 'cause I ain't guilty. I ain't even worried about it."

That closed it. On George's insistence we went back into the jury room with the court reporter and put the offer and refusal on the record in case Seeks went down forever and fifteen years later there was a fight over the possible deal.

Soon, it was on. Folsom was on the bench, Seeks was next to me in civilian clothes, and forty-some odd jurors sat in the gallery. The clerk, using one of those bingo ball contraptions, started calling out numbers. The juror with the number would then walk up to the jury box and sit. Twenty-four numbers were called. Twenty for the main pool, we'd get to strike six and the state two. The other four were the alternates; they'd sit through the trial in case one of the jurors were unable to finish.

Halfway through the numbers, Seeks leaned over and whispered in my ear, "Bingo." Old and lame joke, but a weird time for it. He was either nuts or... well, that's probably it.

IT SAYS HERE...

It was time to voir dire. The Judge asked a bunch of questions about being a felon, knowing cops, hearing anything about the case, and that sort of thing. Occasionally someone would admit to some sort of bias and be dismissed. Then the clerk would spin the cage again and call another number.

Then the prosecutor gets up, asks about people having been prosecuted, having been victims of a crime, and so on. Then I get up, and all the good questions are gone. Nowadays I'm a bit more cagey about this sort of thing and understand by the time it gets to me I'm just trying to get the jury to like me, so I smile and ask questions that are subtle but favorable toward my case. Back then, I just wanted to sit the fuck down. I asked a question suggested by The Chief: whether anyone would be prejudiced because my client couldn't afford an attorney and had to have one appointed.

To this day I don't know why that might be a good question, but it was one I could ask. I asked some other lame questions about reasonable doubt and sat down. Enough of that.

So then we struck jurors. There were a few I didn't like. I struck the three old ladies, and the three mean looking young men. Whatever. Let's get it on.

George then gets up to open his case. He talks a lot about the old lady and it is simple, she says he did it, and why would she lie? Look at how hurt she was, blah blah blah. He says something weird about Winston Churchill which implied Seeks was more or less the Nazi menace. I started to rise to object but everyone in the jury box had that look people get when they hear something they don't understand and suspect they wouldn't believe if they did. Slight squint, mouth mildly agape, and the head tilts about fifteen degrees. So I let it go.

I get up. I manage not to puke. I start stammering about reasonable doubt, then after a minute I start to calm down. I get into the lack of physical evidence, that the woman first said she asked who it was and was told by the robber that he was Tommy Seeks, and so on. For some reason I thought I was being clever by not mentioning her eyesight. I know now that is silly, but so it goes.

We have a little recess after that. I still haven't puked, but I think my not eating may have helped with that. During the recess I sit there and my head spins. Not exactly restful.

Then George calls the Old Lady as his first witness.

Now I know that was a bit odd. At the time I didn't think much of it. She goes up, takes the oath, and we are off. George takes her through the story; I'm writing notes on my cross examination. I don't think I missed any objections. George was rather conservative about that.

What George almost forgot to do was ask his witness to identify the person who attacked her. She kept saying his name was Tommy Seeks, but she hadn't fingered my client. Towards the end George remembered to ask her whether the person that attacked her was in the courtroom. She said yes. He asked her to point him out.

She looked in my direction, looked towards Seeks, then her eyes started to wander around the courthouse. My mind was racing, I was thinking I had something for closing, that she was taking a while to point at Seeks.

Then she pointed to someone over and a bit off my left shoulder. Seeks was to my right. She fingered the wrong guy. "That's him, there in the gray suit."

Everyone turned to look. She had fingered Joel, a new assistant prosecutor. I knew Joel, we were on the Law Review together at Law School. He had recently grown a goatee. He would never in his life again appear in public with a goatee. He did, however, catch a whole load of shit about this from the entire Bar until he left for greener pastures. All playful, but it was pretty hilarious.

George was flustered. "No more questions."

I thought for a second. If I asked questions George could get up and maybe try to rehabilitate somehow, and Folsom might not interpret the "asked and answered" objection strictly and let George get her to finger the right guy.

"No questions of this witness." Fuck 'em. Folsom isn't going to get the chance.

George called the officers. I asked each about finding the purse, or at least grassy shoes. Then I shut up.

George was soon out of witnesses. "The state rests."

Folsom sent the jury off, reminding them not to talk about the case, and that if the lawyers avoided them it wasn't because we are assholes, rather that was his orders. Then he asked if I had a motion.

"Yes your honor," I said as I stood up. "The defense moves for a judgment of acquittal. The state has failed to make a primae facie case of either burglary or robbery against the defendant. The state was unable to establish that the person sitting to my right, the defendant, was the person who committed the offense alleged. In fact, the victim specifically identified another person as her assailant. It is true that she used my client's name, but it is clear that she was not actually referring to my client." I sat down.

"Mr. Clinton?"

George stood up. His head drooped, his chin to his chest. He pushed around a few papers. He sighed. "Uhhh, we believe we have clearly established all the elements of both crimes, that Tommy Seeks broke into the house with the intent to commit a larceny, and that he committed a larceny, stole the victim's purse by means of a physical assault against her." George shrugged, and sat.

Folsom looked a bit glum. "You don't have anything else establishing Seeks as the assailant? Pretrial identification?" Folsom's eyes lit up. "What about preliminary testimony? I could let you reopen the case and..."

"He waived the preliminary hearing, your honor."

Folsom struck the bench with a fist and looked towards the ceiling. "Do you have any ideas Mr. Jobertski?"

What the fuck? I stood slowly. "No your honor, we believe there is no..."

Folsom interrupted me. "Thank you, counselor."

When a judge calls you counselor, that is more or less code for "dickhead." He sighed. "I guess that's it then." He fixed a stare at Tommy Seeks. "I know you did this, you lousy piece of trash. You are way luckier than you ever deserved to be. Just keep one thing in mind. If you ever wind up in front of me in the future, your ass is mine."

Tommy, being a bit stupid, started a reply. "Yes sir, I under..."

"Shut the hell up. I don't need to hear from you." He turned to the bailiff. "Get the damned jury back in here." He turned back to us. "When I dismiss the jury, I want you to stay in the courtroom for fifteen minutes to give them a chance to leave."

While this was going on I wondered if I had a shot at getting the transcript, or whether the end part of this would be tragically lost somehow. I was still green back then; once you deal with judges prone to bizarre behavior a few times you develop a sort of reflex where when the judge starts going sideways you glance at the court reporter to see if her fingers are still moving. If they aren't you, well, try to vouch the record later and see if you wind up in jail or hanging from the flagpole on the courthouse lawn.

The jury returned. "This case has been dismissed,

and we thank you for your service. The clerk tells me that you should call the number given you this Friday to see if your services will be needed next week. The jury is now discharged from its duties in this case."

After the jury left, Folsom sighed. "This case is dismissed. Mr. Jobertski is to prepare the acquittal order. The defendant is discharged." Folsom got up and left the bench.

I stood up and shook Tommy's hand. "I guess you were right."

Tommy turned to go be with his family, but before he could get beyond the bar a state trooper stopped him, turned him around, and cuffed him.

"What the hell?"

"Tommy Seeks, you are under arrest on two counts of uttering. You have the right to remain silent..." and on the trooper went.

After the Miranda deal I got the cop to tell me that there was a matter of two checks stolen from the Old Lady, checks that a bank had taped Tommy cashing. Ye gads. Uttering is when you cash a check you know is forged, so this was pretty strong evidence.

The good thing was the magistrate set a small bond

and Tommy was released. I met with Tommy after that; he told me he was simply guilty.

However, when we talked about it he admitted he thought the checks were rightfully given to a guy he knew for services rendered, and for all he knew he was cashing a check for a friend. Tommy said he took the money from the first check back to the friend, but not the second.

"When I was walkin' back to his car I started wonderin' about him still gettin paid 'cause he hadn't been by the old lady's in awhile. So I asked him about it and he told me the check was stolen. He told me to get in the car and give him the money but I wouldn't do it. He left me there and I walked all the way home and gived the money to the old lady that night."

"Whoa. Where was the bank?"

"Up in North Elm Hill."

"You live down just past the south end by Harris Hollow, right?

"Yeah."

"You walked ten miles."

"I don't know. It was far and was raining. I felt like I needed to get the money back though."

So he wasn't really guilty. Off we go again.

IT SAYS HERE...

The guy who stole the checks was another one of the Catlett Creek crowd. John Shue. It didn't take me long to figure out that he was long gone. Probably took off as soon as he learned the cops were asking about the checks. So no simple resolution.

Next step was to see these security tapes. George made me a copy on DVD so all I had to do was find a DVD player. Back then these things weren't everywhere. So I wound up talking George into letting me watch the thing on his office computer.

The video wasn't exactly thrilling, black-and-white and grainy with about two frames per second. Some guy who looked like Seeks went up to the counter and came away with cash. A shitload of cash.

"Jesus, George. Weren't those checks for like maybe four hundred apiece? He can barely carry the cash they gave him."

"Yeah, lets look at that again."

So we looked again, but it was a shitty video, so really I was just trying to figure it out. I did. He asked for the whole thing in ones. Just the kind of goofy thing Seeks would do. Since he didn't strike me as the strip-club type I figured this was his idea of a joke on the guy for whom he was cashing the check.

"Just strange man," I said. My guy's a weird dude."

George just nodded and asked if I'd been getting in much golf lately. So we talked about that for a while.

My next step was to look for Shue, or at least someone who would admit to having personal knowledge that Shue was anywhere near the old lady, much less that he was known to work for her. The Catlett Creek crowd tended to have sketchy memories and a good sense of when not to be findable.

This was a mild exception. Even the Creek crowd thought Shue was a lousy piece of shit, which is impressive. They all said he did all sorts of work for the old lady and that he would try to sell stuff he'd lift from her house. He'd hit something big and said he was moving to Hawaii. They said he was big on Hawaii for some reason even though he'd never been out of West Virginia as far as anyone knew.

Keep in mind that these folks telling me this and being willing to testify in court to it are two very, very different things. I asked a few of them if they would care to and they laughed like I was joking, and I laughed with them. They made sure to remind me that subpoenas were very, very bad for the memory. At least I knew that Shue was around the lady's house and did work for her. All I needed was someone who would come to court.

I had Tommy's father lined up to testify about Tommy being incompetent to handle his own affairs. His father received Tommy's SSI check and deposited it into Tommy's checking account, from which Tommy couldn't write a check unless his father signed it. That was a good fact as to Tommy's not knowing the check was forged. Tommy's dad also saw Shue around the old lady's house.

I'd rather not have had to use Tommy's father to prove that, but it was looking like that was all I had. Hopefully the old lady would just admit that Shue did some work for her and that would be that. I never make a habit of expecting people to tell the truth, but sometimes I don't have a choice.

A few days later we had a preliminary hearing where I got the old lady to admit Seeks brought her money for one of the checks. In the rain. She also admitted that Shue did some work for her. I figured I had all I needed, the magistrate found probable cause, and the case was bound over.

About three months later Seeks was indicted and

trial finally rolled around. Lo and behold we wound up with Judge Folsom again. There was a brief and ugly battle over my motion to have Folsom recuse himself. Our Supreme Court didn't see all that much wrong with Folsom's threats, finding that it was a reasonable use of a Judge's moral authority to deter crime or some such bullshit. So we had that going for us.

I had two trials scheduled that week, and as the local practice dictated I was to try them one after another. My first trial was really simple; some student down at State was pulled over and the local cops found four small baggies of marijuana in the center console. In West Virginia, possession of marijuana is a misdemeanor, and when less than fifteen grams (as was undisputed in this case) the law requires both a term of unsupervised probation and for the conviction to be expunged after a year of "good behavior," meaning no other legal problems. However, if the state could prove that the possession was "with the intent to deliver," meaning that the person was meaning to sell the marijuana, the offense became a felony. Amount didn't enter into it. Whether the amount was a roach or a boxcar full, the penalty was one to five years in the state pen.

The state was arguing that since there was more

than one baggie my client was obviously a dealer. This is what happens when you have cops totally divorced from the drug culture. One time, a year or two after this case, I had a guy charged with possession with intent and being a pimp. The ground for the pimp charge was that my client mentioned that he and his buddy had "a few ho's with them." The rural cops took that to mean the women were prostitutes.

This case had something nearly as dumb. There was about twelve grams of marijuana total in these baggies, and the officer during the preliminary hearing testified that, according to his "training and experience," twelve grams was not an amount consistent with personal use. I've had friends roll joints close to twelve grams. Cops often just say what they think is needed to win a case. "Training and experience" translates to English as "I have nothing to back this up, so I'll claim I went to a training course and I'm a cop, so trust me."

So we were going to trial. One thing that happened that turned out to be important took place during voir dire. When the prosecutor asked if there was anyone on the panel related to a cop, one younger man raised his hand and said he was the nephew of Corporal Greene. Greene was a not-so-well liked cop, even by other officers. I had a client once that almost ran over Greene while drunk, and once they pulled him over he was expressing his frustration at missing "that asshole Greene." He wound up pleading guilty to the attempted murder of a Police Officer, and was sentenced to six months in jail.

Anyway, this kid admitted he was likely to give more weight to the testimony of a police officer over a regular person and he was tossed off the panel. A few questions later a young lady admitted that she had a family member have some trouble with the law and as a result she held some strong biases against police officers. Off she went.

From there it was a quick trial. The officers claimed that in their "training and experience" the multiple baggies combined with the amount indicated that the marijuana was meant to be sold. It would have been nice if I could have had my client testify, but he was sort of guilty and stuff. So I was left with the standard "potato chip" defense. It worked and the kid was convicted of misdemeanor possession and Folsom just fined him and sent him on his way.

At Tommy's first trial he was in jail so I was able to

direct his attire. I had him in khaki pants, white shirt and tie, all from the collection my office had compiled after years of dressing jailbirds for court. He looked somewhat stable, like someone who a jury wouldn't be afraid to let go. This time he was free, and so all I could do was advise him. I told him to wear something like he wore to the last one.

He just missed. He showed up in camouflage pants, black boots, and a black t-shirt. I gently asked him what the fuck he was doing and was he nuts or what. He answered that he indeed was and wasn't that the whole point? I really didn't have an answer. I was and still am from the school that says you don't want to scare the jury, but I had to admit there was, in this case, possible value to having the jury figure he was too dumb to dress properly.

Frankin County was rural, and as such the jury panel wasn't very large. We only had two judges, so there didn't need to be a whole lot of people to be able to cover both courtrooms. So it wasn't a shock to see both Corporal Greene's nephew and the lady that didn't like cops on the panel.

Except this time when the question of being related to an officer came up, the kid sat on his hands. Pretty clear to me he'd told Greene about what happened and Greene told him to keep his mouth shut so he could get on a jury. Folsom knew damn well what was going on but he clammed up. I let it go, figured I'd grill him about it when it was my turn to ask questions.

Apparently the girl was thinking in the same manner, because when the question about not liking cops came up, she likewise didn't say anything after glancing sideways at Greene's nephew. Folsom was trapped there and said nothing. After that, I didn't say a word about what happened yesterday, I just went through my normal song and dance. George didn't prosecute the case the day before, that was Joel, so there was a decent chance that George didn't know about the girl. The way voir dire works is that there are twenty jurors on the panel, and after we get done striking all those for whom there exists a legal basis to keep off the panel and replacing those jurors, the state strikes two jurors, and then the defense strikes six. That leaves twelve.

I was pretty sure George wouldn't strike the girl. He had no reason to, and more than that the girl was clearly Hispanic. She was the only Hispanic on the panel and for that matter maybe in the whole county. There is a United

States Supreme Court case that says that a party can't strike a potential juror based on race. So if George were to strike the girl we'd have to have a hearing where George would put on the record the reasons for his strike. George wouldn't want to do that so he'd keep her on unless he really had a good reason, like if someone came in and told him about yesterday.

When I got the strike sheet, I saw he didn't strike her. I struck the nephew, and there was no hearing needed because there was no United States Supreme Court ruling keeping me from striking a peckerwood. So I was feeling pretty good about the trial already.

Hell, I even had a decent opening with one of those themes that the people that do continuing legal education classes say you should have but almost nobody does. That there were three chapters to the story, and that the state can only say what happened in the first and last. The first chapter was that someone took some checks from the old lady, and the third chapter was that my client cashed the checks, and in the case of the second check took the money back to the old lady. In the rain.

And off we went.

The state's case was pretty straight. The old lady

admitted that Shue was in her house but she was adamant that she was with him all the time and he couldn't possibly steal the checks, but Tommy was around and she didn't keep track of him. She couldn't have possibly sounded more full of shit if she had hired an acting coach and put great effort into it. She didn't come across as a matronly saint, but rather the kind of batty old lady who scares kids and whose house smells of spoiled milk.

What was fun was the bank witnesses. The same teller cashed both checks, and I got to make a big deal out of Tommy's wanting ones for the first check and how that caused a commotion and it took a while to get ones together and obviously this wasn't the behavior of someone with something to hide. Then the bank officer testified about the loss, that the bank had paid the old lady for the loss of both checks and taken the same amount out of Tommy's account. If you are scoring at home this means the old lady ended up being paid twice for one of the checks. I brought that out in cross-examination.

"You paid her the amount for both these checks?"

"Yes."

"Was she clearly notified as to this payment?"

"Yes"

"Before paying, did you ask her whether she had on her own recovered any of these funds?"

"Yes, we have a standard form she would have filled out."

"Do you have it with you?"

At this point George objected as to relevance, and I was tempted to respond in hearing of the jury that it went to the credibility of the old lady, but I figured Folsom was wise to my jury ringer and would be eager to grant a mistrial if I fucked around. So I asked to approach, and we went to the bench and Folsom didn't give me the chance to argue and ruled against me. I asked to put my grounds on the record and he told me to do it during a recess. So I gave up on her.

Then the state rested.

I was getting tricky in my old age. I had noticed that the checks were from a joint account, apparently Mr. and Mrs. Old Lady. Thing was, at no time during the state's case did the state put on any evidence as to the whereabouts of the Mister. So the state had no evidence that the Mister didn't sign the checks or at least give permission to have the checks signed. The state hasn't proven its case, and we go home now.

I laid that out for Folsom as the grounds for my motion for judgment of acquittal.

Folsom was not happy. He asked George where the Mister was, and George said he's been dead for twenty years. Folsom lectured George for a while about how he should have put on testimony to that effect, and went on about how George fucked up.

Then out of nowhere he denied my motion. "Mr. Jobertski, you are of course welcome to take issue with my ruling with the Court down in Charleston." Meaning that I could appeal. Apparently Folsom's feelings toward Seeks were overriding any sense of legal fairness. He just couldn't bring himself to let Seeks off the hook again. I was shocked.

I put my grounds against the relevance objection on the record, went back to the office, had some lunch, and came back to start my case. I had two witnesses. Tommy and his dad. I put Dad on first, had him explain that his son was a raving lunatic with brain damage, and that he handled all of Tommy's financial affairs. He would drive his son places and sometimes even give the old lady a lift if she needed.

George than rammed his foot in his mouth by

asking Dad whether anyone would be at the old lady's when he would drive her to the store or whatever.

"Sometimes the Shue kid. He did a lot of work for her."

You see, Dad was out of the courtroom for the old lady's repeated shrill claims that she never left Shue in the house alone, and I wasn't the person to ask him about it. It never really occurred to me that it would be helpful. I had tried to paint the father as someone who didn't know what was going on and who wouldn't go out of his way to protect his son, seeing his son was damn near thirty and a pain in the ass and so on. George asking him gave him credibility.

Then again maybe George was just doing his bit for truth and justice. It is easy to start to believe that all prosecutors just want to put people in jail, guilty or no. Maybe George figured the dad would tell the truth and that would be for the best.

So then I rolled the dice and put Tommy on. I really didn't have a choice as Tommy had an absolute right to testify and once he found out that he had to know the check was forged he was pretty fired up about his innocence. I figured that even though Tommy wasn't very bright, he had the priceless gift of being completely self-aware of his own lack of intelligence. I told him to not to bother thinking about what he should or shouldn't say. Just answer the prosecutor's questions honestly and trust me to clean up any mess.

So I called him, and he did an exaggerated limp march to the witness stand. I ran him through his story, about the ones and the walking ten miles to take the old lady's money back to her. In the rain. And so on.

George, bless his heart, tried to trap him and bully him and so on, but Tommy just sat there and answered the questions. Yes. No. Etc.

Then we closed the case. I did my closing referencing my three chapters bullshit, and George sounded more or less how I would sound closing a case where there were seven eyewitnesses, a confession and a videotape of the crime. Muted sound and fury, signifying nothing.

Then the jury went out.

In that town a jury going out would attract lawyers like moths to a porch light. Everyone was walking distance to the courthouse, and usually nobody was immediately busy. So everyone would converge, bullshit, and make predictions. Judge Pope would often walk out and join us.

Folsom almost never did, but he did this time for a few seconds to say hello to a few lawyers. Someone asked him what he thought of the trial and he looked at me and told them to ask me, that I'd know what he was thinking. Then he said to me, "My ruling make more sense now?"

I nodded. It did. Folsom refused to grant my dismissal motion for the reasons I figured, that he didn't want to be the one to let Tommy "We know he killed that kid" Seeks off for the second time. What he was sort of saying was that he would have except I had a ringer juror and the state had a weak case so he was going to let the jury do it for him. The question that never was answered, and sorry to spoil the suspense but the jury came back not guilty, was if Seeks had been convicted would, Folsom have granted a post-trial acquittal motion? To this day I do not know.

Anyway, the jury came back in about an hour into deliberations with a question about the definition of reasonable doubt. The standard procedure for Folsom was to tell them they'd been instructed and needed to work it out the best they could. The funny part about it was that when Folsom asked who the foreperson of the jury was, it turned out to be my ringer. Folsom almost smiled.

The jury came back with a verdict, high drama and all of that. As an attorney when you hear the words "not guilty" the feeling is more relief than excitement. Not guilty means no appeal, not having to have to read a transcript of yourself talking, nobody goes to jail, no self-doubt, no second-guessing.

That afternoon was the last I saw of Seeks. He had the sense to drop out of sight. I search the internet for his name now and again to see if he turns up stalking Stevie Nicks or winning the lottery or something.

Nothing yet, but he had such a Forest Gump vibe to him that I fully expect to see something at some point. I can hardly wait.

III) Breaking a witness.

My office was definitely from the "learn by doing" school. Before my first hearing, a bond hearing in front of Judge Folsom, the main tip The Chief gave me was "Don't worry about it. The Judge will do what he wants and nothing you say will help or hurt. At least not that much anyway."

Bill, the other lawyer, also had a tip for me: "Watch your nuts."

I lived. Bill was there anyway, so if things went wrong I had someone to help me make it a total disaster.

My first time ever alone in Circuit Court was to handle something for Bill in an emergency; I think a bourbon front moved in and trapped him in his house. It was a juvenile proceeding where, according to Bill, all that was left was an "admission" where the kid would admit he kicked his mother and wrecked the house. The agreement was to give the kid probation. Bill told me he had covered everything, the kid understood what was going on and all I would have to do was stand there and nod. No big deal.

Right. So I went to the courtroom and found the kid. Took him into a back room to make sure he knew what was going on. All as planned until I asked why he kicked his mom.

"Because she was standing over me about to hit me in the head with a roller skate."

Hmmm. This means he acted in self defense and it wasn't a battery, and if this kid tried to enter an admission (a juvenile version of a guilty plea) and Folsom asked him why and he said this Folsom was going to be quite cross. So I guess the plea is off.

We go into court. Folsom asks if we are ready. I stand and do all that "if it please the court" garbage and tell him that my client will be unable to enter an admission at this time as he is unable to provide a factual basis.

Folsom shrugged. "I guess we will just have a quick bench trial instead, then."

I'd like to at least know my client's name before going to trial, but sometimes you have to play hurt. The judge told the prosecutor to call the first witness. I have to admit being less than chagrined about the lack of an opening statement. Tricky when you have to look at the file to remember the charges. I look. Seems to be "battery" and "destruction of property." Alright, I'm prepared. Lets get it on.

George calls the grandmother. She babbles, but Folsom likes old people so he's paying rapt attention. She's not saying much, just that she hears things and saw my client kick a door. A picture of the door is entered into evidence, and it looks like it has been run over by the Marshall Thundering Herd. My cross-examination is simple.

"Did you actually see my client kick his mother?"

"No."

From this picture, can you point out the damage caused by my client to the door?

"No."

"No further questions."

George gave me a dirty look. He called the mother, who tearfully told the story about how my client is a little shit and "liked to have broken my leg." Being new to the country I thought that was a statement that my client would have preferred to break her leg, not realizing that "liked to have" in some of the more rural circles means "almost." She also whined about how he wouldn't go to school and an argument about that was when he, being a little shit, tried to kick her shins in.

One of the first things they tell you in Law School is that real life isn't like TV, and for one thing in real life attorneys don't break witnesses and so on.

One of the first things you learn in the real world is almost all of Law School is horseshit.

So I get up to cross-examine this crying woman. Why not just give it a try. Full throttle on the bluster, make myself look tall and mean.

"Now Ma'am, isn't it true that when my client kicked you, you were standing over him with a roller skate about to hit him with it?"

I expected a guilty denial, and then I'd just badger the hell out of her about the exact details until Folsom yelled at me or she tearfully confessed. Helps to have a careful plan. At least that's what they told me in Law School.

Her actual response, however, totally threw me. "Yeah."

Not a guilty "Yeah" either, but more like I asked her if indeed she really had two arms and breathed air. Totally dismissive and casual. All I could do was not blurt out something brilliant like "Really?"

"So you were threatening him, raising the skate over your head in order to strike him?"

"I wasn't really threatening him."

I stared at her incredulously.

"I was really trying to hit him 'cause he was talking back to me about getting up and getting to school," she explained.

"Oh." I considered this, let my brain deal with it for a second; it was just not something I expected. "No further questions."

George had his face in his hands. He looked up. "The state rests."

I briefly conferred with the boy, advised him not to testify on his own behalf. Why bother at this point? He agreed with me.

"Defense rests, your honor."

Judge Folsom lowered his head, mournfully shaking it. He looked up, into the gallery toward the mother and opened his mouth, but no sound came out. He turned his gaze to me. "I find the juvenile not guilty of battery, but guilty of destruction of property and therefore I adjudicate this juvenile delinquent. Mr. Clinton, do you have a recommendation for disposition?"

In the end the kid wound up staying with his uncle and being on probation for a little while. It became obvious that Folsom found him delinquent just to get him into the system and away from his crazy mother. Plus, my client was going to be a sophomore and was a big kid that liked to hit out on the football field, and his moving to his uncle's house meant he would attend high school at Folsom's alma mater, but maybe that was just a coincidence.

IV) I guess this is why they pay me the big bucks

I see that The Chief and Bill are talking about something. Lots of nodding and the telltale head shake and exhale combo that means that someone somewhere in our fair county has done something really fucked up and we are going to get to handle it. So I wander over to The Chief and Bill and ask what the happy news is. They tell me.

Bill was bumming around the Courthouse after magistrate court this morning when a phalanx of cops marched in with rather pissed-off looks. One was crying. It takes some fucked up shit to make a cop cry. So Bill was naturally curious, and started asking questions. The cops had just arrested a guy for some serious child abuse. They say he was swinging his five-year old son around by the kid's penis. Beat the kid with a shovel. That the kid was used as an ash tray. The cops showed Bill the pictures of the kid from the hospital. Bill was a bit in shock, and again, it takes some fucked up shit to make an experienced defense attorney turn pale. I guess this qualifies.

Being an idiot, or at least a nice guy, I recognize that Bill and The Chief both have had children so I volunteer to defend this guy if he winds up being represented by our office. I get no argument. One of those deals where they were thinking the same thing that I was, but they weren't about to come out and say so. I can't blame them.

The next day the talk around the Courthouse is the guy who was swinging his kid around by his penis. I just shrug and plead ignorance. No point in getting into it now.

When I get back to the office I have a new file on my desk, some guy named "Cleetus Minden." I suspect this may be the dick-swinger. So I have a seat and settle in for some interesting reading.

The first part of the file is the initial police arrest report. At the top are the charges. Minden is charged with three counts of "Child Abuse Causing Serious Injury," three counts of "Child Abuse by a Guardian," and one count each of "Sexual Abuse in the First Degree" and "Sexual Abuse by a Guardian." The meat of the arrest report is the narrative.

Cop speak is an odd animal. The idea is to make everything sound routine. It is an offshoot of legalese. In cop speak, nobody goes to work in the morning. Rather you "proceed to your place of employment." That sort of thing. "She said she shot her neighbor's puppy in the ass but didn't kill it" becomes "The white female suspect advised this officer that the female suspect discharged a twenty-two caliber rifle in the direction of a canine owned by an adjacent land owner. As a result a projectile struck the canine in the posterior, causing significant non-fatal injury." One thing about cops: they do get "advised" an awful lot.

This one was a classic in the genre:

> Officer was advised by Southern Franklin Battered Woman's Shelter personnel of a possible abused child. Officer was advised that possible abuse victim's mother appeared at shelter with child. Shelter personnel further advised this officer that possible abuse victim's mother advised Shelter personnel that the possible abuse victim's father was the perpetrator of the alleged abuse. Shelter personnel identified herself as Denise Buxton of 237 Apple Trail, Little Otter, West Virginia. Shelter personnel Buxton advised that Emergency Medical

Services were contacted to provide medical services for the possible abuse victim. Buxton advised this officer that possible abuse victim and his mother were transported to Franklin General Hospital.

Officer then proceeded to Franklin General Hospital to investigate. Officer approached the possible abuse victim's mother. Victim's mother identified herself as Jennifer Brown. Victim's mother identified the Victim as Daniel Brown. After being read her Miranda rights and signing a waiver of those rights, Ms. Brown advised this officer that Cleetus Minden, her boyfriend, had on several occasions struck Daniel with a shovel like object, had burned Daniel with cigarettes, had forced Daniel to sit in scalding hot water, and had picked up Daniel by Daniel's penis in order to swing him around in the air. Ms. Brown further advised officer that Cleetus Minden was arrested for public intoxication last night and this morning she decided to vacate their joint residence to avoid further abuse to her child.

Officer was then permitted to observe the victim, Daniel Brown. Daniel is a white five year old boy with brown hair. With assistance from Emergency Room Doctor Ahmad Hussein, officer observed that Daniel's body was covered with numerous bruises and burns consistent with cigarette burns. Daniel's penis was also obviously injured and appeared to be bruised all over and Doctor Hussein advised that in addition to bruising there were other injuries consistent with those suffered if someone pulled on the child's penis with great force, similar to dislocation with some tissue tearing. Officer was advised that Emergency Room Personnel had taken photographs of Daniel upon his arrival at the hospital. Officer was given copies of these pictures on diskette, paper copies are attached to this report as exhibits. Officer was also advised by Doctor Hussein that as a medical matter an interview with Daniel was not a good idea.

Officer thus proceeded to the Southeastern Regional Jail to interview Cleetus Minden. After being advised of his rights and signing a waiver Mr. Minden advised this officer that he had hit Daniel with a shovel, had burned Daniel with cigarettes, and had injured Daniel's penis when swinging the boy around in the air.

The rest of the report noted that Jennifer Brown was charged with child abuse as to her failure to protect the child. At some point Cleetus was brought up to the Courthouse and arraigned on the charges, where he then applied for a public defender and had his bond set at two hundred fifty thousand dollars.

I assume that Cleetus was then sent back to jail and

the file to me.

What I really didn't want to do was look at the pictures. I knew I had to. I just didn't want to. I surfed the internet for awhile. Slunk off to lunch and played a quick nine at the country club. Then I sucked it up, poured myself about a finger of bourbon, downed it, and then poured a few more fingers and added some water. Then I opened the damn file again.

I guess when you start in this racket there is a natural curiosity about pictures of gruesome injuries. The same part of the human psyche that makes slasher movies economically viable, I guess. However, when you know it is real there is somehow a deeper issue. My "Advanced Scientific Evidence" professor in Law School had us examine some of the more disgusting crime scene photographs available. I guess his idea was that, after that, we'd know if we could handle it, and plus, most likely we would have a hard time being shocked as there weren't going to be many worse photographs.

What he showed us was a charming murder scene. A small bedroom, where two homosexual gentlemen under the influence of methamphetamine were having a little fun when the one pounding the other in the ass (in the biblical sense) decided to hit his partner in the back of the head with the claw end of a rusty hammer. Several times.

Pressure being what it is, the walls were covered with blood, and methamphetamine wig-outs being what they are, the walls were also covered with brain matter because the guy on top kept hammering away even after the skull was quite open. I guess he was climaxing at the time and didn't want to lose the mood or something.

The walls were nice, but the pictures that really were interesting were of the dead guy, still naked, still hunched over on his knees with the back of his skull gone. Maybe twenty photographs, from various angles and so forth. Particularly creepy were the ones where you could see the eyes of the deceased, as his face was intact. I was handling the nausea until the one picture that almost cost me my lunch.

When I say they photographed the body from various angles, I really mean from all angles. The one from the rear, a closeup, caught me by surprise. The dead guy's asshole, reamed open like the Lincoln tunnel, coated with lubrication, semen, and shit. I guess there is the thing that after all I am a heterosexual white boy from a red state, so I'm not a big fan of watching man-on-man butt sex. I don't have a problem that other people are into this sort of thing; it just makes me a bit queasy. Then again, so does broadcast television.

Even with that being said, I don't think it was just the aesthetics that affected me. It was more the idea that this poor bastard was just getting a little action, and not only did this other guy take away his life, but also took away his dignity and privacy so totally that some years later a bunch of students are looking at a full color closeup of his cum stained bunghole as he lies dead and hunched over in an unflattering position on a mattress soaked with his own blood, feces and urine, his rectum wide open for the world to examine.

Even worse, humans being what they are, we are not only looking at the pictures, but laughing at them. Joking about them. Sounds completely awful and morbid, but it is a natural defense to being seized up by something so totally awful that it can't be dealt with honestly. It happens. Better to laugh than to scream, but I'm pretty sure that if the guy or someone who loved him was in the room he would take some rather violent exception.

Just life, I guess. Usually epiphanies regarding the nature of mortality aren't this disgusting or weird, but there you go.

After a while you realize that no matter how blase you attempt to come off as, seeing these things carry a toll. You find yourself manifesting symptoms of stress overload. While the conscious mind can be fooled to where you think you are ignoring it, the wheels are still spinning. Your mind still doesn't like it, and you are hurt by what you see. It is worse for the defense attorney because the natural reaction to seeing these things is to go do something unpleasant to the person who caused them. I don't get to do that. There is every chance I'm going to be trying to protect the person who caused it, to be the one person that takes his side against a vengeful world fueled by rage resulting from seeing something awful, rage that on some level I feel myself but have to swallow and set aside in order to Do The Job. Cost of Due Process, I guess. Somebody's gotta do it. These are the rare occasions where the psychic costs of defending the innocent are less than those of defending the guilty.

All this is much worse when dealing with children. Humor as a defense is out. Laughing at brutalized children in itself is traumatic to the point that it really doesn't help, and is far less acceptable than joking about dead adults, itself not conduct that gets one invited to exclusive society cocktail parties. So you just deal with it. Worse in this case is it looks from the cop's report that the guy confessed, so I'm not likely to be able to get by with the "he didn't do it" thing in my mind. I'm going to look at a badly hurt child, and then go stick up for the guy who did it.

This isn't normal behavior. I know that after seeing the pictures I'm going to want to drive to the jail and kick the guy's ass. The trick is to somehow keep that from affecting the work. I guess some lawyers have a gift of self-deception, that they can be true believers in a cause, no matter how completely fucked up that cause is if you look at it with any measure of objectivity or common sense. I can't do that. I don't want to do that if it means deep down inside justifying the brutalization of a five-year old child.

That is why I'm not wanting to look at the pictures. But I do.

Typical little boy for these parts, a bit inbred looking with the skinny head and the eyes close together, slight of build. The kid had a look of amusement and contentment on his face, his eyes positively shined like a little kid just given a gift. All of this just made his mutilated body all the more disconcerting. His body was covered

104

with obvious cigarette burns. The base of his penis was purple and swollen. The back of his body, from the lower back to his heels seemed to consist of nothing but blisters and bloody, raw skin. All in all nasty, not much worse than much other stuff I've seen, but for the look on the kid's face, the look of a child that doesn't realize there is anything really wrong going on.

This is the sort of thing that can put one into long periods of quiet contemplation as to what "cycles of domestic violence" really mean. I don't know whether I want to drive to the jail and kick this guy's butt or just sit here and feel an eerie sense that at some point, the guy that did this to this child at one point was that child, sitting somewhere with his body covered with painful wounds, not realizing that what happened to him was wrong.

Fuck that. Just do The Job. The prelim is set for seven days from now. I've got to make a little trip to the regional jail and confront evil, or at least the remnant of the very abuse that I'm sitting here trying not to have nightmares about.

The next morning, just a little hungover, I go down to the regional jail. I make the drive, park, walk in the door and for the 453rd time tell the lady in the lobby that my name, office, and bar number is all I'm writing down, that they don't need my social security number or home phone number and I'm not in the mood to create a "steal my identity kit" to be put on file in a jail. Then I sit in the lobby for about an hour waiting for a guard to come tell me that my car keys need to be put in a locker. Then I pass through the obnoxious doors, those doors that when they open make a really loud "crack" sound as the locking device is moved in or out of position. Then I get to sit in a small cubicle with a giant window facing the hall. A faint aroma of body odor fills the room.

I'm a serious non-smoker, mainly because I hate the smell of old smoke on clothes and carpet and so on. However, my jail experience has made me adopt an exception in that I now advocate smoking in jails and prisons as stale tobacco smells great compared to the underlying smell of the jail itself. In this cubicle is a small table and a few plastic chairs similar to really cheap patio furniture except you just know the jail spent at least ten times as much for these. This is where I spend a mere twenty minutes waiting for the guards to find Cleetus. You learn early to bring a book to the jail. Something short and light is best, like War and Peace or one of Kant's knee-slappers.

Finally, I see the guard leading someone who is a dead ringer for Charlie Manson towards my cubicle. The guard points at me and his lips seem to say "there is your lawyer" although I may have missed a few adjectives. The guard opens the door and the Manson look-alike takes a seat. I ask if he is indeed the Cleetus Minden I'm here to see. He is. Up close the only thing really strange about him is the lack of a swastika on his forehead. Other than that, with the shaggy hair, long unkempt beard and crazy shining eyes, he looks real fucking familiar.

"I'm Elbow Jobertski, your lawyer." I figure I'll start off with the obvious. From there the idea is just to get him talking. Learn something I don't know rather than explain to him what I know. I have a carefully crafted question to begin such a conversation.

"So, how they treating you down here?"

This gives a prisoner, especially a new one, the chance to say what is really on his mind, that jail sucks and the guards are assholes and such. Better to start from there and try to slip into the actual case stuff rather than trying to stick to the "relevant" stuff and try to keep him from pulling you into a discussion about the jail. Plus, this usually relaxes him once he gets how pissed off he is off his chest. Just nod a lot and agree, but be truthful. Don't patronize or blow smoke up his ass. It doesn't help.

He lets me know in great detail what he thinks of the jail. Normal stuff about the food and overcrowding. He tells me I need to get his bond reduced. He's also pissed that he is in the sex-crimes pod and that the guards keep calling him "Lester" and other inmates make throat slashing and other friendly gestures when they see him. I'm nodding and murmuring sympathetically. Then he lays a four-star quality line on me: "I do believe that these people is prejudiced against me."

I slip in a little gentle honesty. "Well Cleetus, you are charged with sexual abuse of a small child, so it makes sense that they may not like you a whole bunch. Plus, didn't you confess to this deal?"

His eyes bulged out of his head with my first sentence. "I ain't no fucking pervert and I ain't ever done no perverted stuff with the boy, I ain't touched the boy outside of a little spanking when he stuck a pen in my neck and I sure as shit ain't told nobody anything different. What you talking about I confessed to this shit?"

"That's what the law is saying, that you told them

that you beat the kid, burned him with cigarettes and swung him around by his penis."

"Bullshit!" He yelled, eyes in full crazed Manson mode. "Fucking cops are lying on me!"

I shrug. "They claim they have a tape. I'll get it and see what it really says. Anyway, they say that the mom and kid say that you did all of this, so to be honest we are in some deep shit either way."

He just stared at me with a look of guilty panic.

"So, are you telling me you never hurt the kid?"

"Yeah. I spanked him once is all, when he stuck a pen in my neck. He once ran into my cigarette when I was smoking it, but that was once and he wasn't hurt bad."

"O.K. I'll look into everything. One more thing, Cleetus. If you want to help yourself you need to do something for me. It may sound strange, but it could mean the difference in your case. You listening to me?"

He nodded soberly.

"Shave and get a short haircut. Right now you look like Charlie Manson and the judge and a jury aren't going to like you much."

"Who's Charlie Manson?"

Sigh. "Some guy who was famous for killing a

bunch of people in California back in the 60's. Not the guy you want to remind anyone of, so shave and get a haircut." I swear, if the next words out of his mouth were "What is California?" I would have, well, cried for starters.

"I'll think about it. I don't want to look stupid."

I shrugged. "If you would rather be in jail forever than look stupid, I guess tha's your call."

He just looked at me blankly.

"I'll see you in a few days at the preliminary hearing. Maybe we can get that bond reduced and get you out of here."

The preliminary hearing was an odd day. I had two cases on my calendar, Cleetus Minden and some misdemeanor fleeing from an officer case. Officers don't like it when people run. I don't think I'm giving up any secrets there. Officers also like to sneak in a pop or two on someone that runs. Adrenaline gets the better of judgment for a few seconds. For the most part, if they don't go overboard nobody cares, and more often than you think this includes the guy who was beaten.

I'm supposed to be some sort of liberal and all, but I'd joke about half-seriously that maybe there should be some standards. If a guy makes you run on foot on open ground an officer gets one punch. Through the woods he gets two. So on up through a high-speed chase through a residential area, which allows the officers the full Rodney King treatment.

Transparency is the key. All of these have to be videotaped of course. Plus this avoids the officers coming up with some bullshit "assault on a police officer" charge to justify a fictional self-defense claim. Win-win all around.

I know. Sorry.

I talked to the client and his main complaint was that the officer wasn't in uniform when he ran from him. State law says the officer has to be wearing his funny hat, and that officer wasn't so he had every right to run.

So I go to the officer and the officer laughs. "Yeah, I wasn't wearing my hat when I chased him."

"Okay, what's the catch."

"I went over to your client to ask him about his possibly being drunk in public, and I guess your client was worried about something, so he knocked my hat off and took off running. He made it maybe twenty feet before I tackled him. I think I could get him on a battery of a police officer, but if he just pleads to the fleeing I'm fine with a fine. I appreciate a man that can think on his feet."

So that one got worked out.

The Minden case was a little different. Most of the time a preliminary hearing is waived for a bond reduction or some other goodies. None of that in this case. So we have a hearing.

The hearing consists of the officer more or less describing the injuries inflicted on the child and that the child blamed Cleetus. The officer was the one doing the interview, so I asked him if he had any specific training on how to interview children.

Nope.

That about summed it up right there. Probable cause was found, the motion for a bond reduction was denied, and the case went into pre-indictment limbo until the next grand jury term, about two months away. During that time I brought another bond reduction before the circuit court, also denied rather aggressively. So I did some research into the interviewing of child abuse victims and the pitfalls of an interview done by someone without training. I interviewed Cleetus a few more times; he wasn't all that helpful. He just repeated that he hadn't been home in a few days and never hurt the kid.

I couldn't do much more because I wasn't entitled

to discovery until Cleetus was indicted, and without that I really didn't have any details. So it all went on the backburner.

Meanwhile, there were all sorts of fun diversions. I managed to get a pipe-wielding maniac off on a technicality. To be fair, he was probably a maniac; I don't know for sure. Mainly what happened is that the indictment was specific that the battery happened on March 15, and the prosecutor kept asking questions about February 15. I kept my mouth shut. It was one of those trials where there were two defendants, so there was another attorney involved.

For some reason, he got up to cross-examine the state's only witness, the victim. I tripped him before he could get up. I made it look kind of accidental, but I basically leg whipped him, asked for a recess, and asked him what the fuck he was thinking? Why give them a second chance on re-direct? He understood, and the case eventually was tossed.

He limped for awhile after that, but I didn't like him all that much so I didn't care.

Eventually Cleetus was indicted for a few things. Three counts of child abuse causing serious bodily injury, one for the swinging, one for using the kid as an ashtray, and one for beating him with a shovel. A count of sexual abuse of a minor by a parent, for the dick-swinging. A count of sexual abuse in the first degree for the swinging. All of this added up to eighty years maximum, with parole eligibility in seventeen years.

The arraignment went through without any problems. I finally got my discovery, and was extremely interested to read the transcript of the interview to see if the cop did anything suggestive or otherwise foolish. I wasn't disappointed. The tape with the child was amazingly bad. One exchange summed up the whole mess:

Cop: So when daddy grabbed you by your pee-pee...
Kid: No. Mommy.
Cop: ...you were outside, right?
Kid: No. Mommy. I was in the bathtub.
Cop: That isn't what your mommy said. Is she a liar?
Kid: No.
Cop: So daddy grabbed you by your pee-pee...
Kid: No. Mommy.
Cop: Do you like ice-cream?
Kid: Yes.

Cop: When we are done we can get some ice cream. Would you like that?

Kid: Yes.

Cop: So, did daddy swing you by your penis?

Kid: Yes.

I guess the cop forgot what was going on and instinctively tried to dig out a confession. He went the rest of the tape badgering the kid for the rest of the story. A normal person listening to it would figure out that his mother was the one hurting him, that she burned him in the bathtub and yanked him out by his penis, that she used him as an ashtray. The shovel thing, however, was him, but there weren't any physical injuries from that. Just a spanking with a fireplace shovel, not likely to make one parent of the year, but not worth ten years in prison either.

The interview where Cleetus "confessed" wasn't much better. He denied everything at first, but then the cop dragged out the tired but true technique of rationalizing the conduct.

Cop: Come on now, Danny was being a brat, wasn't he? He probably needed a beating, right?

Cleetus: He did stick that pen in my neck that one time, and I spanked him pretty good. I guess I used the fireplace shovel, but I don't think he was hurt much, no marks or anything.

Cop: So you did beat him with a shovel, right?

Cleetus: I guess, if you put it like that. I wasn't hitting him with no long-handle shovel or anything. I just spanked him a bit.

Cop: What about the cigarette burns. Did he deserve those too?

Cleetus: I ain't never done nothing like that.

Cop: Couldn't be an accident?

Cleetus: One time I think he ran into a lit cigarette. I was just sitting in a chair you know, and he came running by and hit my hand. He wasn't burnt bad by that. I seen the pictures you shown me, and I ain't never seen him burnt up like that. It's that crazy bitch. She did the same thing over in Washington Cou-

Cop: So you might have burned him once or twice.

Cleetus: Maybe once, but not like in the pictures.

Cop: But you did it.

Cleetus: If you are gonna twist what I say like this I guess I best get a lawyer.

IT SAYS HERE...

Cop: You sure? I'd have to arrest you if you did that.

Cleetus: You going to do that anyway. Get me a lawyer.

Cop: Okay.

(end of tape)

So at this point I'm not exactly sold on his guilt and feeling like a bit of an ass for the way I felt when I was first assigned the case. I was really curious as to what the heck he was getting into with the Washington County stuff. It looked like she'd abused someone before but without details I'd never figure it out, seeing Jennifer Brown didn't have a criminal record for child abuse, just some petty drug stuff and a DUI. There might have been an abuse and neglect proceeding where Jennifer might have lost custody of a child or something like that, but these weren't a matter of public record.

So back to the jail I go. He explained to me that seven years before she had permanently lost her parental rights for her two kids because of the same kind of abuse, and that she had accused her then husband of being the abuser before being caught out because it turned out the husband had been arrested in another county and was in jail during the time she claimed the abuse occurred.

117

I had dates and names. I tried to find the husband, but he apparently had shot himself soon after losing his parental rights because the child services people claimed he failed to prevent the abuse. He didn't have family anywhere I didn't need a tank to get to, and I didn't really have anything to ask them, anyway.

The next step is to call the Washington County Courthouse to see if I could find someone dumb enough to maybe confirm that an abuse and neglect file existed for Jennifer Brown. It would be easier to get the judge to go along with my desire to push this angle and help me get access to it.

Some things turn out to be easier than they sound. When I mentioned Jenifer Brown's name, the silence on the other end was telling.

"I guess you know of her?"

"Yeah, she's a psycho freak that beats on kids and blames other people."

"She's at it again over here in Franklin County. I'm a lawyer representing the guy she's blaming."

"I'm not supposed to give you the file."

"Of course not. I was just trying to see if it was there, not waste anyone's time."

"Oh, I'm not supposed to give it to you, but I'm gonna, anyway. She's evil and I don't give a shit. Just don't admit where you got it from. Can you just pick it up though? I have to log everything I send in the mail and I don't feel like leaving a trail."

"Sure. When?"

"Can you meet me at the Huntington Mall in an hour?"

"It's a three hour drive, how about then?"

"Okay. In the food court. I'll be the one wearing a red shirt with a big file on the table in front of her."

"Fair enough."

I love this cloak-and-dagger shit sometimes. I think it kind of turned her on, the whole weird sneakiness of it, but I was married back then and am a pretty faithful guy. Completely faithful, but whether that is my being noble or just to lazy to want to keep lies straight I don't know. Either way, I flirted a bit and went home.

While getting my hands on the file was fun, I was faced with another one of those double binds. For the sake of my case, I wanted whatever was in the file to be as nasty and sordid as possible. On the other hand, I really would rather that something that nasty and that sordid not have happened to a kid. I guess this is one of the pitfalls of thinking too much.

The file didn't exactly disappoint, except as to my feelings about human nature. At least I was now allowed to feel some sort of righteous anger towards someone, as Jennifer Brown was clearly as evil a woman as has walked the earth, if you believe in evil. I don't for the most part, but this woman was clearly a danger who needed to be kept away from children.

She got in trouble in Washington county over her first kid, a girl. Same story with the cigarette burns but no scald marks; obviously no penis pulling, though. The kicker being that this kid was almost completely disabled with cerebral palsy. The medical records indicated she used the kid as an ashtray for about two years before she got caught out. A social worker basically forced her to allow the kid to go see a doctor given concerns about her condition, and when the burns were found Brown went all weepy about how Dwane Brown, her husband, was doing all of this and threatened to kill her if she said a word. Eventually they found that some of the burns were less than a day old and Dwane had been in jail for three days when the abuse came to light.

She lost her parental rights, which meant that when Daniel was born someone should have removed him from her clutches as quickly as possible, but I guess she slipped through the cracks. She was never prosecuted for some reason, but I figured I had enough to force something to happen.

I set up a meeting with the prosecutor assigned to the case and told him he might want to bring his boss, the elected prosecutor, along. They had been demonizing Cleetus in the media, or at least what passes for media in Franklin County, every chance they could get. He was the rubber chicken de jour, to be stomped on as an example of how the prosecutor's office was keeping the streets safe and so on. I really wasn't thinking of this meeting as a chance to shock and embarrass anyone. I just wanted to help those poor bastards off their high horses as gently as possible lest they decide to choose political expediency over justice. They and a wannabe tough judge could go a long way toward keeping all my pretty evidence out of court. The best way to win a trial is to not have it.

My idea was we'd quietly get Cleetus a cheap bond, they could shut the fuck up about the case, and once the flames went out drop the damn thing. I was willing to listen to something like a misdemeanor plea for the shovel seeing he'd already had done enough time to cover it, but wasn't thrilled with it. After a bit of back and forth, that is what happened. It all sort of petered out. They wouldn't go after Jennifer because it would have called attention to their wrongheaded claims about Cleetus, so she escaped and is probably somewhere torturing puppies or something.

Yeah, not exactly a stirring ending, but I wasn't in the drama business. They deserved to be embarrassed for not listening to the interview tapes rather than taking the officer's word. If they had done that they might have looked into the mother's past and put a psycho behind bars. Cleetus was happy to get out of the mess, and that is where my scorecard ends.

V) "When the going gets weird, the weird turn pro" (Hunter S. Thompson)

It's sort of like inflation, the way you look at things. At first something like an attempted murder is a big thing. Several years later you find yourself saying things like "It was just a regular triple execution style murder during a robbery, but the weird part is..."

You tend to lose the neophytes there. The ones that really can't wrap their minds around how a triple murder can be "regular," much less when it is execution style. Not to mention the extra dimension hinted at.

Too many dead bodies, is what it is. Too much pain. Too many absurdly awful events. Next thing you know:

"Weird case, kid stabbed an eight year old boy to death."

"What's the weird part?"

"That he had sex with the corpse afterwards."

"Oh. Up the ass?"

"Nope. Stuck his dick in the stab wound."

"He come?"

"I'm afraid he did."

"Yeah, that's weird.

After that sort of nonsense, the kid blowing his stepfather's head off over an argument about truck keys is not really worth writing home about. Not that your parents really care to hear any of it.

The videotape of the guy boning his own son is alarming until you see the one where some guy is making his six year old daughter use a stun gun on his genital region. Then the regular molestation starts to hit that "normal" phase as well. It takes someone getting up pretty early in the morning to shock you after that point.

Stupidity becomes routine as well. Some guy gets into a drunken argument while drinking out in the middle of nowhere and shoots someone. The guy drives home, or tries to, and deposits his car in a ditch. At some point the guy gets in his head that maybe he didn't kill the guy. He calls a cab and has the cab take him to the scene. Guy hops out of the cab, puts a bullet between the eyes of the guy who as it turns out was dead already, and then hops back into the cab. The now completely freaked out cabbie drives the guy home, hoping that the guy doesn't realize he's an eyewitness to this whole mess. The drunk gets out, the taxi drives away and gets the cops over the radio.

I would love to have heard that exact conversation.

Oh yeah, the cabbie was in shock and unsure where he dropped the guy off. So his identity was in doubt until he called the taxi company and told them their driver took off before he could pay. Gave them instructions to his house.

Which is kinda dumb.

The odd thing is that upon hearing the story my reaction wasn't along the lines of "What the fuck!!! Holy shit!!!" It was that from a technical legal standpoint the guy was guilty of the attempted murder of the same person he had already murdered hours before.

I used to think the story where a guy is busted for possession of illegal drugs, gets the case tossed for an illegal search, then goes to the police station to demand his property be returned and is again nailed for possession was an urban legend.

Used to. Not anymore. Usually they just call you

and ask if they can get the drugs or guns back. On rare occasions they take matters into their own hands and wind up down at the station demanding their property back. It does happen with guns more than drugs though. Felon in possession of a firearm, I get the firearm suppressed, same story.

Sure, you see the occasional eye-widener in civil practice. Like the one "hostile work environment" suit I saw. Guy has a vasectomy that goes wrong, which is bad enough right there. Thing is, the guy is then either blessed or cursed with sudden and uncontrollable iron bar like erections. He has a job not dealing with the public, and his employers also let him wear, er, comfortable and roomy pants.

The kicker being that the guy is hung like a horse. So he's walking around and now and then he's pitching a ten inch tent for no reason.

This is the sort of thing that catches people's attention. Maybe inspires the odd remark. I guess the guy got way too tired of hearing things like "Wow!! Do you have two coke cans in your pants or are you really happy to see me?" and decided to sue.

I have no clue how that turned out. Most of my civil

IT SAYS HERE...

cases had to do with wild things like the standard deviation of the curvature of steel beams. I got to write exceptionally detailed letters to clients and insurance companies, letters nobody read, I'm sure, but they looked good and I could bill for them. Or more to the point, they could bill for them. I was basically selling myself out by the year to people that then sold me by six-minute increments.

It paid well, but I wanted better stories to tell.

VI) Eight Dollars

The arrest report said that my client beat up some 18 year old kid over some dispute. According to the report my client told the arresting officer that "I was just sitting there in the car with my girlfriend and this punk comes up to the car, slaps eight dollars on the windshield, and asked me if that was enough money for me to let him fuck my girlfriend. So I beat the holy dogshit out of him."

That would fall under the "confession" category as far as the merits of the case go. Might help with sentencing. I'm in the lobby of the courthouse waiting for my client, whom I've never seen before as he was apparently way too busy to come in for a client interview. Some skinny kid wanders in. I ask him if he is my client. The kid tells me that he is the victim. Since this kid is about five and a half feet tall and maybe a hundred pounds if he is carrying something really heavy, self defense kind of disappears as an argument unless my client is really tiny or this kid is the redneck Bruce Lee. I'm also a little concerned that the kid looks like he had been hit by something rather large, like the '85 Chicago Bears. That or his mother ran out of cloth and wanted to practice sewing on his face.

I go back to the magistrate's office and see a few deputies standing around. I make some small talk and figure out they are there for my case. So I ask them what the deal is. A little secret about petty criminal work is that the cops are the people running the show. The prosecutor is too busy to care all that much so most of the time he is going to adopt whatever opinion the cop has. So finding out their thoughts can shortcut things a bit, let you know where you stand. Since in this case my client has more or less confessed the whole thing boils down as to what kind of sentence these guys want and where that leaves me with wrangling with the prosecutor.

They have no good news for me. They do have a few pictures. Not happy pictures though. These are crime scene and victim photos. The victim photos are just awful. This skinny kid laying on a gurney, with what looks like his face in an indescribable expression of total pain and anguish, the kind of face that you just know this kid was wailing for his mother. That is if his mouth was physically capable of delivering a wail. He looked like he had been in a pie fight, but with deep dish pizzas.

More disturbing was the photo of the scene. It suggested one word only: Antietam.

They then tell me that in fact had a local woman not wandered down that road the kid would have likely just bled out. It appears my client, after beating the kid unconscious, drug him to the side of the road and just left him there. Some lady happened by that mostly unused road looking for her dog when she saw a foot sticking out of the bushes. She called for the ambulance, and here we are.

What I can't figure out is why we are dealing with a misdemeanor. The deputy reads my mind. He tells me that he really doesn't know either, and has half a mind to just dismiss and take it to a grand jury. I put that little tidbit in the back of my mind as something to keep in mind as to plea bargaining. My client wants to have a felony roughly as much as the prosecutor would like to deal with another felony case on his docket. So the only question here is jail time. The cops want at least six months. They are wholly unimpressed by the "eight dollars" story, partially because of how bad the kid got beat up and partially because they figure it is bullshit. I chitchat with the officers a little while longer and wander back out to the main lobby.

Sometimes people in these kinds of cases just don't show up. About once a week someone just decides not to bother, or figures if he moves to Texas nobody is really going to care so much about a misdemeanor that they will extradite him. I go take care of a routine DUI case and when I walk back into the lobby I see a person that I both figure is my client and really hope that I am wrong. Guy is about six foot tall, can't guess a weight but I can say he is ripped. Thickly muscled, bulging biceps, that sort of thing, with chiseled features. To top it off he is accompanied by two blondes which are by local standards both flashy and attractive.

I walk up to him and confirm my fear that he is my client. I direct him into an empty room so that I can at least have some idea of his story. I ask him what in the heck is going on, more or less in those exact words as I am not really a believer in beating around the bush. He explains that yes, he hit the kid, but in self defense.

I looked at him incredulously. "So, what color was the bazooka he was holding?"

Blank stare.

I explained: "The kid you beat up has been pretty much destroyed and he was a lot smaller than you. Unless you want to claim he was holding some kind of serious weaponry I'd counsel against a self-defense claim. Not so much that we are going to lose, as much as because I'm gonna go out on a limb and maybe say that you aren't the kind of guy that likes to be laughed at."

Blank stare. Blink. "O.K. then, what about what that little shit said about my woman? Are they going to cut me a deal 'cause of that?"

I sighed. "I don't know yet, I need to see if the prosecutor likes it, but the cops don't seem to be moved by it."

Eventually, the prosecutor got to that case. He looks at the file, chats with some cops, comes over and tells me he will take a plea to six months. Otherwise he's dropping the case and taking it "upstairs," meaning that they will just get a grand jury indictment and try my client for a felony. I start working him a bit.

"What about the crack about the eight dollars? I bet anyone would have taken a swipe at that little shit. You would, wouldn't you? I mean, I've seen your wife...."

He cut me off. "What thing about the eight dollars?"

Lets just say that most rural prosecutors aren't big fans of closely reading the file. I point out the relevant text of the police report to him. He starts laughing. "Shit man, I'd have done the same thing. Let me go talk to the officers."

At this point I might as well start humming the theme to "Jeopardy." It all depends on a conversation in which I have no part. Just wait, look through my other case files, stand around like a dork, that sort of thing.

Still waiting.

The prosecutor returns. "The officer seemed to have jogged my memory about something a year or so ago. I think your client may have the bad misfortune of having this happen to him before. It wasn't my case. I'd remember that. I'll tell you what, come with me to the file room. If it is a new story I'll go to thirty days. Not new, still six months."

So we go to the file room, and he talks the clerk into doing a search for our boy's name. Comes up with a few hits. One is a misdemeanor battery. So we find the actual file. Inflation must have hit. The last time he kicked someone's ass it was because the person offered six bucks to fuck his girlfriend.

"What a coincidence" I exclaimed. "Poor guy, having such things happen. At least the price is going up. How 'bout just letting him walk?"

George grinned back. "Sure, in six months or so."

So I went off to tell my client the bad news. He could do six months in the regional or he could wait a few months and probably wind up doing two to ten years in the state pen. He wants home confinement. He just got this job, you see.

Home confinement is one of those ways the system tries to reconcile all these new crimes that require incarceration while at the same time trying to not spend so much tax money on jails. You can only triple bunk prisoners and feed them crap to a certain extent. It was getting to the point of total absurdity. One time I was at the jail talking to a client who had, at the beginning of the conversation, told me he had been tossed in solitary confinement. About fifteen minutes later he made a reference to his cellmate.

"Whoa. Cellmate? Aren't you in solitary?"

"Yeah, but they're double-bunking that now."

Which is surreal. Another exchange had to do with

134

the mats the jail would issue the new prisoners that would have to sleep on the floor. I asked the client if he was sleeping on a mat.

"No." He replied.

"Really? You have a bunk already?"

"No. They are out of mats."

To try to keep the jails from bursting at the seams, someone had the brilliant plan of just slapping a tracking bracelet on an ankle and making the prisoner stay in the house when not at work, church or engaged in any other absolutely necessary activity. Cheaper for the state, and in theory better for the prisoner.

Except that in reality most people on home confinement got there through drinking or other substance abuse, and part of home confinement is that the Sheriff's boys can drop in whenever for a sample of your pee. No drugs or drinking, no slipping off to the local bar or even a friend's place to dodge the wife. It was not unheard of for some good ol' boy, a week after being "hooked up," to show up drunk in the parking lot of the Sheriff's office asking to be taken to jail because he can't take being in a no-exit pit with his wife any longer.

Anyway, this means I get to go see George again,

ask him a question when I know what the answer is. Still gotta ask though. "How 'bout letting him save y'all a few bucks on jail fees while contributing to the tax base? He has some kind of real job and..."

He cut me off: "I'll tell you what. Since it is a Wednesday, and I like Wednesday, I'll stand silent as to home confinement and let you ask the magistrate."

While it sounds big of George to do this, it really isn't. The magistrate is as likely to allow my client to serve his sentence on home confinement as I am likely to be asked to serve as the next Pope.

I'm not Catholic. She's not a fan of home confinement. She could be convinced to go along with a prosecutor's recommendation, but none of that. Thus, I get to play the fool again, tell the poor bastard that it is up to the Magistrate.

"She makes the call if you plead guilty. No way of knowing the answer beforehand, except that I know she fucking hates to put people on home confinement for some reason. Do you have proof of employment? If not, I doubt she even considers it, not that she's going to be thrilled either way."

"Sure. Here is the guy's card. I start Friday. You

136

think she might give it to me?"

"Honestly? Or do you want me to blow smoke up your ass?"

"I'd appreciate the truth. Be a new thing to hear from a lawyer."

"She is simply going to look for a solid reason to deny it. If she can't find one she will deny it anyway, most likely. Except then we have some chance of appeal. You sure this is a real job? She will check and if you are lying, this could get ugly."

"Yep. Up and up he hired me and I start Wednesday."

"Well, you want to try it this way? One thing I can do if she shoots down the home confinement is to ask for six months and a day. That extra day makes you eligible for good time and work credits. Six months is six months. Six months and a day comes out to more like three and a half months."

"If the prosecutor will recommend the extra day I'll plea."

So I go off and pitch that to George. He's all for letting my boy work off some time and he really hates having trials, so he agrees. Off we go to plead in front of the magistrate.

Actually, we first have to complete a written plea. So I take the guy into a side room and go over a carbon form that says I've explained six months of advanced constitutional law to him in 10 minutes so he knows all the wonderful rights he is waiving by pleading guilty and that the recommendation by the prosecutor is just that and if the magistrate wants to bend us over she can and all that other happy horseshit.

After that, we go into the magistrates office. Those innocent of the system are usually shocked by the casualness of the whole thing. No courtroom. Just the magistrate's office. People are usually sentenced to terms of up to a year in jail with far less ceremony and deliberation that buying a used car. We just slide in and I say that there has been a deal reached, that in return to a plea of guilty to battery, the state is recommending a six month and one day sentence, minimum fine, and will stand silent as to allowing the defendant to serve the sentence on home confinement. The prosecutor says that this is an accurate account of the agreement. She then asks my client if he wishes to plead guilty. He says he does and we hand over the written plea. All there is to it. He's now convicted of battery in the State of West Virginia.

Ahhh. Magistrate Pam Older. She is basically a slightly more reasonable version of Judge Judy. Takes no shit from people but doesn't get too crazy with power and generally can be reasoned with. She squints at me. "He have a job?"

"He tells me he has work lined up starting Friday with this gentleman's company."

Note that I say "he tells me" instead of stating this as fact. This is what is known in literary circles as "foreshadowing."

Magistrate Older smirked. "Hmmm. Did you tell him that I would check?" She looked at my client. "Are you lying to me?"

"No ma'am," he said, polite as the day is long. "I know you would check and I sure wouldn't try to lie to a judge."

Always a good idea to call a magistrate a judge. They aren't, but a little over-respect never killed anyone.

The magistrate grabs the phone and starts dialing. Looks like a mining equipment company in the next county. "Hello?"

"Yes, this is Magistrate Pam Older in Franklin

139

County. I was calling to confirm that a certain individual is employed with you..."

"Really?"

"Thanks. Sorry for the intrusion."

She hangs up the phone and shakes her head in disbelief before fixing my client with a look of total bewilderment.

"Are you by any chance retarded?"

"Um..."

"That wasn't a question you are supposed to answer with anything but a tearful apology or a damn good explanation for why you both lied to me and thought that it would work."

"Umm... Didn't he say..."

"What he said was that he has no employees anymore. He's been out of business for a month now and just happened to be in the office trailer getting drunk."

My client just stared at the carpet.

The Magistrate rolled her eyes. "Yeah, that's what I thought. Just because you have the sense to shut up I'll not give you the maximum. In fact, I'll even give you less than recommended just so there are no hard feelings. Six months flat."

Thus ensued a spectacle where my client pleaded for more time and the Magistrate refused to give it to him. The arresting officer led him away to be transported, I put the copy of the sentencing order in the file, and life moved on.

VII) Where were you when....

The next day is one of those nice days outside. Clear blue sky, nice and cool. Perfect day to walk in the woods, maybe play some golf, or go try to defend some petty criminals in magistrate court. I'm down with the latter. I'd never do the first one. My position on that is if you ever see me outside without a golf club in my hands I'm looking for the door to get back inside.

From the file this case looks really dumb. Complaint filed by city cops, one of those small cities that is pretty much a village with an ego. These kinds of towns usually can't attract officers that have had proper training. Most of them have no experience and are hired off the street because they were turned down by Wal-Mart. There is some statute on the books that allows a city to hire uncertified police officers for two years; after that they either go to the academy or find other employment. So most of these towns just keep people for two years at minimum wage, then find someone else.

So the quality of work is at best spotty. At worst it is hilarious. Mostly it is alarming.

Today I've a case out of Baldwin, one of those really small towns with moron cops. I've a history there, and due to their history of abject stupidity I've declared a "no tolerance" policy toward cases filed by that force and vow to never let them convict anyone. One time I had a guy accused of violating a protection order. His story was that he approached an officer and told him he needed to go to the house where his ex-girlfriend lived to get some tools he needed for work. He wanted no trouble, and wanted the officer to go with him or maybe even to go for him. The officer said no problem and offers to drive the guy there. Once he gets to the house, my guy goes into the garage for the tools.

The officer sits in the car. When the guy returns the officer arrests him for violating the order. The ex-girlfriend sees the whole thing from inside the house and confirms this. Thing is, so does the cop. He's too stupid to see the problem.

So we aren't dealing with Serpico here.

I take a peek into the file. Obstruction of justice. No real narrative. Cop just says that the suspect interfered with the officer's duty. No mention as to how he interfered or what the duty was. Not exactly helpful. The arrest warrant was signed by the city mayor. In these towns that job pays very little, and isn't exactly held by the town's brightest bulb. More like the town drunk. Usually it is a toss up as to whether the guy is more stupid or corrupt. This one is currently under indictment in federal court for some kind of scheme where the city court (he acts as the judge) would reduce DUIs to reckless driving and not tell the Department of Motor Vehicles about it so that the defendant wouldn't have any license trouble. This was usually in exchange for a small gratuity.

You just don't walk into the magistrates office and get to business. First you have to sit in the office, engage in the "how are you" and "what is going on" type conversations. There are about twenty cases on the docket in front of two magistrates, but since there is only one attorney we have a bit of dead time to just bullshit about things. Mainly local gossip and general news stories.

"Hear about the plane crash?" She asks.

"No, I don't see a whole lot of news when I'm here. Where at?"

"Some plane just hit the World Trade Center."

"Weird. What kind of plane?"

"Don't know. Just heard from the officer."

"Didn't some plane hit the Empire State building years back? Maybe something like that."

Older shrugged. "Maybe. So, what's up?"

I tell her I've got what looks to be another Baldwin saga. She sighs. "So what's the deal."

"Obstruction of justice. I'm gonna go ask the officer what the deal is. So far I can't tell what was obstructed."

So I go find the officer. He tells me the story. I try to keep from laughing. This one's a keeper.

I meander back to Older's office, a look of merriment on my face. I plop down in a chair. "This one's a classic."

Older shakes her head in a gesture of "Jesus Christ, what this time?"

"So I ask the cop for the story. He says that he gets a call from Deputy Jones that he has a eviction notice he's to serve on my guy and whether this cop has seen him. So the cop says no, but he'll keep an eye out. So the cop then spots this guy in some convenience store, and he then calls Jones on the radio. The cop then goes up to him and says there is an eviction notice that is to be served on him and that he's to stay there."

Older interrupted me. "An eviction notice is civil. He can't hold someone based on that like an arrest warrant."

"Exactly. But it gets better. My guy apparently knows this. So he asks the cop if he is under arrest. The cop says no. So my guy starts to leave. The cop jumps in his way. My guy asks again. The cop says no. So my guy goes into another aisle. The cop jumps in his way again. Same question, same answer. My guy used to play tailback at State. So he puts a little 'fake right go left' on the cop and gets out the door, and walks with some urgency towards the county line about a block away. He knows he won't get served over there. The cop gets in his way again. He asks the same question, gets the same answer. Finally after a few of these my guy gets right to the line. At this point the cop arrests him for obstruction for both dodging the service and not heeding his orders."

"That's completely insane."

At this point an officer flew in through the side door. "Another one."

"Another what?"

"Plane. Another plane hit the World Trade Center."

I exhaled loudly. "I guess it wasn't an accident, then."

Usually during these momentous occasions we like to think of ourselves appreciating the weighty reality of the moment. You remember where you were, but later the fact that you were doing anything but standing jaw agape at the awesome power of history seems embarrassing, as if it were an offense against decency. At some point it would sink in. It took a while. There was some commotion and speculation about what kind of plane. Up until the officer clarified we'd mostly assumed it was some kind of Cessna type plane. Wrong.

147

The prosecutor stepped into the room. Steve's ex-military, made law review. Came here to open an office and is part-timing at the prosecutor's office to help with the startup. "Lets get through this shit and get out of here."

"Have you talked to the cop in my case yet?"

"No."

"Try it. A shot of levity into your day."

Exhale. Slow blink. Head lowers and shakes back and forth slowly. "Fuck."

The Magistrate calls out as he leaves: "Even if you dismiss I want to talk to the officer. Get him in here."

I go off down the hallway. The halls are usually full of cops and attorneys standing around bullshitting waiting for their cases to come up. Not today. They are all down the hall in the crappy lounge watching a crappier 12" television probably manufactured during the Ford administration. No cable, black and white, snowy picture.

On the screen is the World Trade Center, a hazy picture. One of the towers starts to crumble and fall. A hush falls over the room. I walk back down to the office as not to miss the prosecutor's return.

"One of the Towers just crumbled." I mention to

Older on the way in.

"Good Lord."

The prosecutor returns. "Jesus. He told me after telling the story that he wouldn't demand jail time if the guy pled guilty. I explained to them that the realistic deal would be if they dropped it maybe the guy wouldn't sue them. We are dropping the case."

Older nodded. "Bring him in here anyway. I want to have a little talk with him."

As the prosecutor left, he had to dodge Bill coming into the office. "The other Tower just collapsed."

"Figured. Anything else going on?"

Bill grinned. "No. Just that. Slow day."

The prosecutor led the officer into the office. Smoke then started to come out of Older's ears. "Can y'all leave and let me have a word here?"

Bill and I went back to the lounge. We could hear Older yelling something but couldn't make it out. In the hallway one of the Elm Hill officers was sitting in a chair, playing with his service revolver. Spinning the barrel, etc. Very weird thing to do in a courthouse.

I stopped. "Howya doin' there Carl? Look a little frayed."

"Jesus on a stick. Someone knocked down the World Trade Center. Someone crashed a plane into the Pentagon. I heard a car bomb just went off in D.C. next to the justice building. What the fuck? Gotta be them fuckin towelheads. We gotta bunch of em' down in the valley goin' to State. I see one near my house I'm shootin' the fucker."

"Um... you been up a while there Carl?"

"Yeah. Had the night shift and had to come into court. Man is this one long fucking day,"

"Hey man. Why don't you go back home and get some sleep. If the State guys run amok I'm sure someone will wake you before they get far."

He squinted at me. "Elbow, I do believe you may be fucking with me a bit, but you probably right." He labored into an upright position. "I ain't doin' no one no good like this." He shuffled towards the exit. "See ya."

"Bye." Bill and I continued back to the lounge. The room was empty, but the TV was still on. Still the news. Now it seems a plane crashed somewhere. "How 'bout this shit?"

Bill shrugged. 'I can't help but wonder if in the end this is going to mean that the next time some cop just fucks with someone he's going to get away with it because some jackass politician uses this to scare the hell out of everyone."

"Man, you may have set some kind of conference record for cynical introspection there. Right past the disaster to the aftereffects. Nice."

"That's why they pay me the big bucks."

"What about all the dead people?"

Bill shrugged. "Welcome to history."

The TV was still showing the talking heads, shots of the building, people covered in dust and soot walking down the street. There was a news crawler across the bottom of the screen. The words began to catch my attention: "The chemical plants in the Kanawha County area of West Virginia... ." My wife works near there. Those plants are bad news. One of them is pretty much identical to the one that killed all those people in India back in the 80's. So it was a mildly stressful wait through the commercials. "...Are on alert." The message ended. Whew.

We work our way through the rest of the docket.

Mostly drunk driving cases where pleas are worked out without much debate. Obvious facts, officer here, plea to minimum fine and 24 hours. Back a decade or so the Federal Government told the states that if they didn't make jail time mandatory in drunk driving cases then the state could kiss a bunch of highway money goodbye. Nice idea, hold the tax dollars of the state's own citizens hostage unless the state does what you say. The lesser known kicker is the constitutional right to an attorney kicks in whenever someone is facing jail time. So now the states get to spring for a lawyer for every DUI involving a poor person. Most of the time the public defender, who is not paid by the hour, advises a plea bargain in an obvious case for minimum punishment. Then there are the appointed counsel who are paid by the hour, often lawyers in need of a few bucks. They tend to be a bit more "aggressive." Adds up.

VIII) On the edge...

So I have this client charged with second offense driving under the influence and second offense license revoked for other than driving under the influence. To save the suspense, he's guilty as hell. No real argument about that. There is a videotape where he, slurring and stumbling, tells the cops that he was weaving because of the boil on his ass. He then, on the tape, shows the cops the boil. To this point, I thought "showing your ass" was just a bit of country slang, but I guess you learn something every day. Plus the officers have the DMV papers on hand about the license. He's guilty there as well. He knows it and wants to plea. He didn't bother to make bail and just sat in jail waiting for the hearing. It is all time served. He's an ideal client. Nice guy who just needs to stop driving drunk.

The only drama is as to the sentence. The DUI 2nd carries a mandatory six months. The license infraction carries a mandatory fifteen days. He's not getting home confinement. He was on it before for something and was one of those guys that decided they liked jail better than having to stay in the house with the wife. Therefore, the only question is whether the sentences will be consecutive, or end to end, or concurrent, meaning they run all at once.

Sounds simple. Except for that whole good time and work credit thing that only applied to sentences greater than six months, which requires some basic math skills to figure out. I know that, contrary to common sense, if the sentences are run end to end my client will wind up doing about twenty days less time. Poor George doesn't really know what the deal is, whether the extra fifteen days are greater than the good time benefit.

He asks me about it. I shrug and say I don't know. George has a chip on his shoulder about drunk drivers for good reason. He's been in a nasty accident and lost a family member. He wants whatever results in more time. I know that, and since it isn't my job to help him I just claim I don't know. I figure Magistrate Older is going to do whatever he recommends and I figure if he guesses I have a fifty-fifty chance of the lesser sentence. High drama.

We go before the Magistrate and enter the plea. My client is contrite and candid about his crimes. Older asks George for a sentencing recommendation.

This is when George for some reason pulls out a coin. That night he wound up in the hospital for a kidney stone, so in retrospect maybe he was a bit over the top with discomfort.

"Heads concurrent, tails consecutive. Sound good to you, Elbow?"

I'm stunned, but this seems about par for the course. The client is losing it, but I make eye contact and a gesture of reassurance and he calms a bit. I figure it is a figurative coin flip as to which way George would go with sentencing, so why not a literal coin flip? I nod my assent to George.

He flips the coin. It hits the ground, rolls toward the Magistrate's desk, and damned if it doesn't roll up against the desk leg and come to a rest on its edge.

I didn't miss a beat. "I think that's an acquittal, isn't it?"

IT SAYS HERE...

George is just stunned. My client is totally bewildered.

Older is unimpressed. She rolls her eyes, thanks me for my recommendation, and sentences him to consecutive terms. Looks like the figurative coin flip came in after all.

George is still a bit freaked. I offer to buy him lunch. He says he needs to go see a doctor. At the time I figured it was some cryptic joke. I tell him, "Don't worry, it happens to all of us at some point," referring to his failure to flip the coin. He just nods and walks off.

I shrug and go back to the office.

IX) It is all in the timing.

Then there was the time I inadvertently converted a whole holding cell into born again Christians. It was just a normal afternoon of preliminary hearings. During these hearings, all of the smiling defendants who were unable to make bond would be massed in a set of three holding cells in a larger locked area. Having a client back there is a pain in the ass for several reasons.

First of all, it is in this locked room in the back of the courthouse. Seriously locked, like with one of those huge keys and a big metal door. Until you casually try to catch one of these things with a foot or a shoulder you can have no real idea how much these doors must weigh. So you have to go flag down a deputy with a key and get the deputy to open the door.

Then, you are confronted with three more doors,

solid steel except for a small window about six feet off the ground, and a slot in the door about eight inches high and thirty inches wide. Through this is where you conduct your business. This slot is about three feet off the ground, so you can either crouch over or squat. Very comfortable. At least the client can sit on one of the benches lining the particular cell. You, on the other hand, get to work your quads and lower back.

So you get to squat and try to discuss what to do with zero privacy as the other denizens of these cells don't have much else to do, and they are probably tired of discussing French poetry with each other. So they listen. This by itself makes things a bit dicey. What makes it usually absurd is that this captive audience generally is not sufficiently entertained simply by listening and usually will give in to the urge to participate.

So when you are trying to advise your client, he's also getting a ton of unsolicited advice from at best questionable, but passionate, sources. Some of the advisers really deep down inside think they are helping. Why the client would think that the person stuck in the cell with him somehow knows dick about how to get out is anyone's guess. But that is how it works.

IT SAYS HERE...

As background, the legal purpose for a preliminary hearing is to determine whether "probable cause" exists to believe that the defendant has committed a felony so that the state can keep the guy in jail or on bond pending a grand jury indictment. In this context "probable cause" can be met by an officer reading his report, or maybe having a victim make an accusation. So the practical purpose of a preliminary hearing for a defendant stuck in jail is to trade the preliminary hearing for a lower bond. Prosecutors would rather not have to go through hearings. Makes them late for tee times. Plus putting some of the witnesses on the record makes it hard for them to change their stories later.

So when I'm in the back squatting down trying to explain this to some guy, there is also a chorus telling the guy all sorts of weird things.

"He wants you to waive your rights? Fuck that. Don't ever waive your rights. He a public defender. They work for the state like the cops. He a cop man."

Or...

"Thousand dollar bond? Ask him for a PR bond. My lawyer gettin' me one. My cousin got one when he was arrested." (A PR, or personal recognizance, bond means that the defendant does not have to post any money, he just promises to show up.)

In the former instance, usually the client has given two confessions and was on videotape committing an armed robbery. I've negotiated the bond down from $100,000 to $5,000 with a 10% cash option, meaning that he can post $500 and get out, but now he's getting the Patrick Henry treatment from some random car thief. In the latter more or less the same except the adviser is in for something like forgery and my guy is in for malicious assault and a thousand dollar bond would be the lowest ever set for a like crime in that county. But his buddy the prescription forger is helping him keep it real and not get fucked over by his idiot "Public Pretender."

So I'm trying to convince someone to not do something stupid while someone stupid tries to get him to do something stupid. This can be frustrating. Jailhouse lawyers are an occupational hazard. The bright side is that the holding cell variety of the species is mainly a nuisance. The prison variety tends to be simply mind-blowing. They have more time to figure out reasoning that they should be let go even though they pled guilty to murder because... well, I have no idea. They send you 34 page briefs citing a hundred cases and manage not to make a lick of sense. The jailhouse guys just babble. They don't have the time to figure out how to argue night is day by stringing together out of context sentences from case law.

Some guys fuck with you on purpose. They do the exact same things the earnest guys do, but when the client turns to you with that confused look, they make that "hand over the mouth trying not to laugh" look. Sometimes these guys will stop it if you call them on it. Sometimes they just act offended that you suggest such a thing and this proves you work for the state, etc.

Meanwhile, there is this pain in your knees...

On the Day of Conversion, I drew the rarest of audiences, the helpful kind. There was a very large black man in the cell. He was bald with a large round face, a face with a spaced out grin. He assured clients that their attorneys were telling the truth. He'd also talk a lot about Jesus.

My client that day was your basic, standard-issue crackhead. He was in for possession with intent, busted selling a twenty dollar rock to a confidential informant. Since that makes him a "crack dealer" and I'm in a county of silly white people, his bond is set higher than it would have been had he beat the informant with a crowbar. I'm back there feeling my knees start to hurt, discussing the bond and what amount he can raise and what I can get it down to and the helpful guy is reassuring my client, and we reach a reasonable reduction request I can take to the prosecutor.

So I go back to the courtroom. Usually there are about twelve cases set at 1:30 P.M., so I'm waiting around until the prosecutor on duty gets to caring about my case. I forget who the prosecutor was. I do remember that the officer didn't show for the hearing, which made it impossible for the state to establish probable cause. So the case gets dismissed.

When I get back my client is on his knees in front of the jolly moon-faced guy. I can hear the moon-faced guy say: "Get up and sin no more brother. Do not let Satan steal your joy, brother. Jesus loves you and... ." I figured if I didn't interrupt I could be there all day. I got my Johnny Bench on, caught moon-face's eye and asked him if he converted my client. Moon-face beamed, my client turned towards me with a confused look on his face. I shrugged.

"I guess it worked then. The officer that arrested you didn't show up so the state just dismissed your case," I said. They will release you as soon as you get back out to the regional so they can give you your clothes and stuff."

I walked out of the holding area, hearing the other prisoners' chatter about my client going loose and just as I left I heard moon-face start in a booming voice, "Brothers, let me tell you... ."

One person's miracle is another person's lazy cop. I'd like to think that finding religion would make my crackhead suddenly stop toking, find a job, and..

What, exactly? He was a crack addict. A week later he was trying to sell enough to be able to get what he needed to smoke. This time he was in a car and sped off when the buyer flashed a badge. The cops knew who he was and didn't chase. They usually try not to get into high speed chases, but the crackhead didn't quite realize he was clear and tried to run over a tree two blocks away.

He detoxed in the hospital while his broken pelvis, cracked ribs, and shattered arm healed. When he was finally healed enough to be arrested I talked to him at jail. He asked me about getting some help for his obvious problem. His detox made him far more aware, and I guess this sort of experience changes things even for a fiend. As part of a plea I arranged for him to attend a secure facility while awaiting sentencing. He wound up going to prison for the distribution of cocaine, but he went sober. He was one of the few ones that I saw after he got out. He stopped me on the street one day about three and a half years after the Day of Conversion, I didn't recognize him at first; he weighed a bit more and didn't look confused. His teeth were still a mess though.

"Remember me?."

"Weren't you the guy that got converted in the holding cell that one time?"

"Yeah." He shrugged and scuffed his shoe on the pavement. "I went to church and shit that weekend. That big dude told me that prayin' and shit would keep me off that crack. I tried but... ." He trailed off.

"But the tree, prison, and those N.A. meetings are working a whole lot better for you."

"Yeah. Funny thing is, I can't bear to even think about going to church no more. Makes me nervous and upset and gets me thinking about that damn crack. My momma tell me I'll go to hell if I don't go. I tell her I 'ready been there and I'm going back if I go to Church so I'll take my chances with the Lord."

I nodded, smiled, and we parted ways.

X) Of course, there is the issue of race...

The first time it happened had nothing to do with the law. Actually it kinda did. I made my first try at law school at a school out of state for reasons that are both obscure and mildly frivolous. I can say if my then girlfriend's pet rat had waited another day to die things would have been much different.

I hated law school the first time through. Actually, I wound up liking law school, I just hated the idea of being a lawyer. I didn't mind being in the Midwest all that much, except for the whole flatness and geometrical nature of the Midwest. I did get lost quite a bit. Elevation changes strongly inform a hillbilly's sense of direction, and I never really got into checkers.

I just wasn't emotionally mature enough. I came out alright as far as grades went the first semester; I just wasn't all that thrilled with the competitive nature of law school, people that would hide books and not want to discuss things with you as not to break some sort of weird study group ethos. Okay, in some ways I was probably too emotionally mature.

Us versus them, and in that place I was definitely "them." I just didn't have a demographic. It was a private school, one that I would have never attended without a tuition waiver. Mostly rich kids with lawyer, or otherwise professional, parents, kids that thought "The Paper Chase" was a contemporary documentary.

The "study group" was the main social unit. Five to eight students united with the goal of, well, I'm not sure. They would study together, share notes, refuse to help anyone else, and silently calculate how to knife each other. A bit grim. My status as being some sort of scholarship case was well known, and I was invited to participate in several, and kicked out of all. The first two because, not being a fan of the particulars of the law school social structure, I accepted an invite to be in a second study group. This made me a traitor to group one and two.

The third bounced me when they figured out my undergrad majors were Philosophy, Math, and Drama. Only pre-law was acceptable; I would be behind on the learning curve. The last one was mutual. We were going along fine, but I would commit the terrible sin of working with students that seemed to be struggling and asked for my help. Ultimatums were issued, I refused, and sic transit me. Res Ipsa Loquitur.

So I wound up a free agent. I'd work with whoever wanted help. I just couldn't quite grasp the nasty competitiveness. I'd always learned more when dealing with people who needed my help or when none of us had any real clue and had to dig it out of the dirt. After a while, the edge came off of the whole thing and the parties started, which made up for everything. I was still outside, but tolerated once I managed to handle being "called on" in class very well.

That is the crucible of law school. Being "called on." Most professors will just pick a name at random and torture that student with questions about a case. Then another question about that answer, and on sometimes for the whole class. This is known as "Socratic Method," after some Greek who so annoyed his contemporaries by asking questions that they made him drink a glass of drain cleaner. I guess it is just the sophisticated version of the three-year old asking you "Why?" and then repeating the query after every answer. Except the three-year-old is a malicious academic with twenty years experience, a post-doctorate degree, and very possibly a hangover.

Acquit yourself well, and you earn respect. Completely bomb-out and you are the law school equivalent of a leper.

I guess this is because the grades don't come out until the end, and until then the only data to feed the hyper-competitive need for measurement is how well one stands up under this grilling. It can get a bit ugly, especially when it involves someone who got straight A's up to that point and is used to giving right answers and that being the end of it. In this arena the right answers just inspire even tougher questions. Add that to the fear of failure produced by knowing the stakes, and wild things happen. I've seen people just get up in the middle of this and run out the door, never to be seen again.

I loved this atmosphere after I came to terms with it. I wasn't emotionally invested in becoming a lawyer. I just went because I took the LSAT on a lark and received a rather large score, and what else was I going to do? I could go hustle golf and play poker, but why not at least get a straight skill? Acting was a bit too spotty and I wasn't about to try to move somewhere where I could do it. L.A.? Fuck that.

Others had their identities so intertwined with being a lawyer they could see life no other way. It was life or death. Not the death of the body, but of the person this silly bugger always wanted to be. They'd discuss law all the time. They'd read only books about law. Discuss legal opinions not so much regarding the law but about the personalities of the justices and blah blah. At first the overpowering sense of fear rubbed off on me. I gained weight, started drinking more, all of that. Until I sat down and thought about it. Then it became a delicious absurdity. I started losing weight. I kept drinking, though. We all did.

The parties now seem the stuff of legend. Fridays usually started with some kind of social deal sponsored by some organization. This was more or less a kegger in the basement. The first one I figured was going to be one of those sip at a half-cup of beer with my pinky sticking out while discussing something or other with faculty members and other students.

I could have been more wrong, but I doubt it. They sold cups to drink with, I guess a way to stick handle around the idea of just selling booze, seeing I usually don't pay five bucks for a plastic cup. These cups were large, like a quart large, and there were usually at least five kegs for maybe a rolling total of one hundred fifty people. Pretty much everyone got hammered and discussed something or other. Not law. It was like the beginning of the release of a pressure valve. Law students were soon drunk enough to socialize with non-study group members, talk to the professors, and, weird as it sounds, talk about things other than law.

By about seven the kegs would be close to dry, and then there was a lull where people sort of retreated back to core parties. There was a guy in my building who had a fully stocked bar in his apartment. I became a partner in this and contributed to the booze. He was about five foot seven, and weighed like three-fifty at least. If he got into an argument at a bar with someone he would be sure to quickly insult that person by calling him "fatass." We got along quite well.

Between five and fifteen people would wind up back in his apartment. Nobody ever went to my apartment, at least not before 3 A.M. I was taking slob to a whole new level; I broke a glass in October and instead of cleaning up the glass I just quit walking in that part of the apartment until January when I borrowed a vacuum cleaner. I also accidentally set fire to part of the rug in a broccoli-cooking accident best left not described.

We'd drink and throw darts, watch TV, listen to music, but mostly just drink. Darts were a big thing there. One thing that never even occurred to me until I left that school was that there were no drinking games. Just drinking. Mostly mixed drinks, all sorts of weird crap because this guy was a bartender, but way too many Long Island Ice Teas. One of the few clear memories is tasting one batch, and saying with all seriousness: "Too strong. It needs more Tequila."

After a few hours of this, there would be a bigger party at someone's rented house or whatever. Most of the first-year students lived in either my building or in a neighborhood of student rented houses referred to as "The Ghetto." This is when the tension completely released, with predictable results. Very Dionysian. Particular memories are a bit of a blur, but the air of release was borderline orgasmic and something impossible to forget, something

I've never experienced since. When I went back to Law School years later it wasn't there, mainly because there just wasn't that much tension.

I came out alright the first semester. Top ten percent or so. That was when I started to look into what I could do with a law degree, and I didn't like the answers. I really figured it was a waste of time. I finished the year, partially out of a sense of duty, but mainly because I'd a year's lease and not much else to do in the meantime. So I sort of studied and enjoyed the whole scene. The spring semester exams I decided to just get over with as soon as possible. Most law professors, and all the ones at this school used time pressure as part of the exam, maybe two or three hours as well as limiting the length of an answer to a blue book or two. Pressure. So I figured I'd beat them at their own game and really tear through this stuff. A portion of us all met at a bar afterward to commiserate and then after a few drinks begin to work on the next one. I'd just get drunk as I really didn't care that much.

The last exam was Civil Procedure. The maniac Professor allotted four blue books and set a time limit at five hours. I was done in about forty five minutes and half of one book. I caused laughter when I turned it in. I was somewhat drunk by the time any other students trudged into the bar. That was the night the tension completely broke, and... well.

I wound up with a C+ on the Civ Pro exam. Stayed in the top third of the class, and washed my hands of the whole thing.

Which gets me back to the first time. Classes ended in early May and I had the apartment through June. I had an acting gig in some dinner theatre place in the mountains as the understudy for all five of the guys in 'Waiting For Godot," but not until July. I guess if two or more actors blew a rivet I'd be two or more characters at once. I pointed that out to the director, who told me he'd seen worse adaptations than that, something about mutants in trash cans. Thankfully that didn't happen. I just worked on scenery and helped out. For years I could still perform all five parts at once, which was a rather unappreciated talent. Except for the one time it got me laid, but that's too weird a story to get into now.

So I'm stuck in the Midwest for about six weeks and I'm low on funds.. Paid summer internships for law students were hard to find, and I was sick of all that to boot. So I went to a temp agency and got work for $9 per hour as construction labor.

It wasn't bad. I was part of a labor crew headed by a guy named Sheldon. Five guys. All but Sheldon were new that day. All but me were black, and by Friday all but Sheldon and I were gone. It was some serious work. I relished the brainlessness and needed the exercise. When I showed up the next Monday with three other newbies, I had seniority and Sheldon, who had an urban patter I had began to understand, started calling me 'The Dog Catcher" for some reason. I was afraid to ask why.

When I was still there the next Monday, Sheldon said I was a credit to my race. Of course Sheldon had been doing it for about two years and sometimes went to do landscaping in the evening. Mainly I'd just go home and hurt. Or play basketball.

That was one hell of a week. The elevator broke down. We were building a hospital, five stories, three of which were done. We were putting up drywall on the fourth at the time. The labor crew would clean up and carry heavy things around when needed. As the elevator broke down, there were heavy things that needed moved. Like all the drywall sheets up to the fourth floor. Which was all we did that Monday. Sheldon and I were the only ones in the crew left after lunch. Eight hours in all of carrying drywall up stairs with a half-hour for lunch.

I knew pain that night. The next morning it took ten minutes to get out of bed. I managed to walk the five blocks to the site on time, mainly because I wanted to see Sheldon's face when I showed up. We did it for another eight hours. Up the stairs, legs on fire, arms sore, back aching. We'd get the odd ten-minute break and talk about pussy. At least I think we were. When I got back to my apartment I threw up. I slept for twelve hours, drank a bunch of Gatorade, and went back to the site.

Sheldon laughed when he saw me. He said he would have called off but he wanted to see if I'd show. Eight more hours. Still haven't fixed the fucking elevator. We wound up moving the last of the sheets at about three-thirty. Quitting time was at four, so we just hung out around some carpenter types and talked. We were sitting on a bench, the other guys were putting tools in tool boxes and so on, and one asked Sheldon how he was doing.

"Damn," he said, shaking his head. "They workin' us niggas way too hard." Then he looked at me and laughed. "Yeah Dog Catcher, after that you a nigger too. I makin' you an honorary nigger. Work the white right off yo' ass. "

I just smiled and thanked him. I wound up quitting that job after Friday, and became the first person ever to give any notice, albeit about four hours, that I wasn't coming back. I had enough funds to carry me home before the job, I was working for drinking money at that point and had quite enough cash to last me. I would have probably kept at it, but on Friday morning we were hooking up some scaffolds near the edge of the fifth floor. Somebody slipped into me and knocked me towards the edge. I reached up and grabbed the crossbar of the scaffold. I looked down as my body swung out over the five story drop and then, what seemed like hours later, back over the floor so I could let go. Fuck that. I gave my notice and found something to sweep up for a while.

While I was drinking one night the next week I got to talking to someone who turned out to be a contractor about how hard it is to find help. I told him about my experience, just bullshitting. He started grilling me about Sheldon, and as I understand Sheldon didn't show up the Monday after that, probably being the first construction laborer ever headhunted and money-whipped into changing jobs.

Weird fucking world.

After I came back to Almost Heaven and went through what I swore was my last acting gig, I started... well... I don't know. I played poker for about half my money, bet on college football for a bit, and rented myself out as a hockey goalie. You see, there are a lot of people that like to play hockey but not so many want to goal-tend. Often they are practicing but have only one real goalie on the squad, or just need a goalie. This is where I would come in. It was fun and a few bucks. I also did some mathematical consulting work. I managed to avoid doing local TV ads. I admit to doing a few radio ads.

It was fun for a while, and then some of the poker pigeons decided that a pair of kings wasn't a great hand in seven card stud hi-lo without a declare and I figured I might actually do something else with my life. What killed me was a business deal. I had been negotiating to buy a building that needed a little work. I had gone back and forth with the agent and the six heirs that held the property, slow-going because all six would have to agree and so on. We were about set on a price when some idiot came out of nowhere and makes a firm offer for twice what I was offering.

IT SAYS HERE...

So then I was really sick of that stupid fucking town.

I had set up a deal where I was going to go to the University of Manitoba to get a doctorate in African History. The literature said to dress warm. I didn't major in history, unlike the three majors I finished I was one class short, one I couldn't fit in. But I'd taken several African history and African Lit courses. The lack of written history interested me greatly, as did identifying Eurocentric constructs and how they impact the conception of this and that and then actually create tragic effects and so on. Well, that and the idea of a West Virginian going to the middle of Canada to study African history was the sort of thing I'd do just for the hell of it anyway.

Then I thought better of it and went back to Law School, this time at West Virginia University. I was sick of hockey.

So I went through all that and started a job in a (for here) big firm and learned how money can be wasted in bushels. Complex mass tort litigation. A complaint that took fifty pages or so just to get to the "v." Firms charging a quarter per page to copy documents for clients, then faxing a copy (buck per page) so they have it right away.

One partner noting that the fax machine "was the most profitable associate in the office." I was bothered that soaking clients by profiting off expenses wasn't so ethical, so I was a bust for them. They had even paid me a signing bonus, I was the Law Review can't miss next big thing. Eight months later I knew how Ryan Leaf must have felt. Or would feel, anyway.

I wound up in a public defender office, where I got to be a lawyer and didn't have to wear a ski-mask all day.

I had to do some city court duty for a town in the really rural county I first worked in. City court would start Wednesday about eight P.M., and end about ten. We each took a town. I got stuck with the largest one, which wasn't saying much. The same guy was the judge in all of them, and his legal knowledge was a bit spotty. He was mainly a court-cost collector, and "guilty" was just something that needed to be said before he got the money. Kind of like a little kid saying please to get a cookie. The town prosecutor, who would be one of the county guys moonlighting for a few quid, and I would just go hash over the file and decide if the guy was guilty. If he probably wasn't the prosecutor would just get rid of it. If he probably was I'd get a plea offer for a five-dollar fine and two hundred fifty dollars in court costs. If my guy didn't take it, we'd have a jury trial. The offense didn't matter. Any real crime went to the county system. The city was limited to giving 20 days in jail and weren't about to spend the jail costs, so these were all fine deals, except that jail time was possible so they had to drag me in on it.

The way we picked a jury is the judge told an officer to go up to the burger joint on the corner and get ten people. We'd voir dire them and if there were more than six left they'd let me strike some to wind up with six. Then it would be a fiasco, seeing the judge knew no law. He was either the mayor or selected by the mayor and I think he had to be a high school graduate, although I'm not even sure about that. We had the opening and the closings and the witnesses and so on. I'd make ornate evidence objections just for the hell of it. The Judge would ask the prosecutor whether I was right, and sometimes the prosecutor would ask me what I was talking about and then wind up agreeing with me about it. Very weird.

The jury instructions were on the order of "If you think this here boy done, lemme see... caused an offensive and unwanted touching to this here other boy on purpose, then you can find him guilty of battery." I'd saunter over and whisper something to the Judge. Then he'd continue: "Oh Yeah, that's right. Y'all got to have no reasonable doubts either, y'all hear me?"

Then he'd be found guilty. I'd make a passionate plea for leniency and a fine. Once I knew the game I was using quite a bit of my drama background.. The Judge was great. He'd hem and haw about how the defendant "needed some jailin'," and then he'd tell the guy that just because his lawyer did such a good job pleading his case he'd let him go with a ten dollar fine and five hundred bucks in court costs. I'm not kidding about these amounts. The fine went to some statewide fund while the city kept the court costs, and those coming up with these amounts had mamas who were strictly no voters as to the raising fools issue.

Anyway, one Wednesday I didn't have anyone scheduled to be there. Sometimes they'd call at the last minute. Since I liked to stay on the good side of the judge I'd hang around the office until eight. I'd go play some golf at the club, get a shower and come back and play around on the computer, Civilization II or internet poker or something. About nine I'd figure they were good without me and I'd make the trek over the mountain into the valley where I lived.

This day, the call came. Whoops, they missed a battery and this guy is an asshole. I deal well with jerks and troublemakers, although I can't fathom why. I remember one old guy going nuts over his son getting arrested, he said his kid did nothing and why can cops get away with this shit, arms waving and spit flying.

"Because people vote Republican," I blurted out for some reason.

The old guy nodded and calmed down. "Yeah, I reckon that's it."

So I'm here for the battery. Someone hands me an arrest report. Racial deal. Punched some black guy in the head; the victim asked the cop to keep it local, doesn't want a hate crime mess. They want the twenty days on this one, and tell me to let him know they just might have to let the county make it a felony if he doesn't like it. He's over in that room over there.

I go in and sit down. Skinny nasty looking redneck type. Old jeans, flannel shirt, worn denim jacket, and a confederate flag hat. He's looking at me like I've four heads. One for each of his teeth.

"I'm your court appointed lawyer. Have you seen the..."

He cut me off. "What the fuck. Are you fucking kidding me?"

"Umm... I'm sorry sir, is there a problem?"

He was raising up and leaning away from me. "Fuck yeah there's a problem. You think I'm gonna let a nigger be my lawyer? Get the fuck out of here!" He yelled this, spitting out the slur.

I admit I was a bit confused. "But." Words failed me.

"I'm not?" Still not really registering.

I stopped. I exhaled. I shrugged. I looked him straight in the eye.

"Fuck it." I said, and left. I went out into the hall. The judge and prosecutor heard the yelling and looked at me about half-confused and half-amused. I shrugged. "Well, do you think we can get Bill over here? Maybe he can pass for white."

They took that one to county court and charged the felony.

Race has always been a weird thing for me. I'm pretty darn paleface, or at least close enough for government work considering all the Seminole ancestry.

So what that guy was screaming about is anyone's

guess. Maybe he knew about Sheldon.

I grew up in West Virginia in an all-white area. Race was mostly an abstraction. You would hear really stupid racist jokes and garbage like that. "I think God makes people black because they did something wrong in a previous life" wasn't something I heard from some guy burning a cross. It was a teacher. I really didn't buy it, because Willie Stargell was black and he was the greatest. But my teacher told me this. My teacher. The authority figure. Yet some years later she had a "Jesse Jackson For President" yard sign. Which made some sense at the time. It really did.

Mainly I'd wind up just arguing with people about it. They'd ask me if I'd "let my sister marry one" and then I'd point out that was none of my business, my older sister could do whatever the fuck she wanted and given the law of averages it would likely be an improvement on the guy she was with now. This would of course filter back to her boyfriend, who would not be very amused by my comments. The upside was I learned how to fight, mostly how to take a punch. I spent way too much of my time fighting off bigger kids who would beat on me for being a "nigger lover" whenever the subject came up. I also learned to run.

Which again, was all in theory seeing our entire community was white. In effect, I was getting beat up for not agreeing to hate people I didn't know for reasons nobody would explain. Or at least I quit asking after my teacher laid that bit of country wisdom on me. I did wind up in the County Library trying to figure out why some people were white and some were black, and think I figured it out that God had little to do with it. Problem was, I started wondering what God had to do with anything, but that's a different story.

It still never occurred to me why anyone really gave a shit though. My parents would just shrug. Other kids would respond in a tautological fashion and we'd wind up in the principal's office. The books would tell me that a lot of people did, but not why. It was like there was some secret that nobody was letting me in on. As I got older and entered the larger world I'd be paranoid that I was acting oddly in some way any time race was an issue. At least until I was in college for about a month.

I was visiting a friend at his college and wound up getting really drunk. I got pretty lost and happened into the lounge of a dorm where there were about ten guys shooting pool, all black. Somehow we wound up having a rather frank and open discussion about race; you can imagine how that would have gone. After a while of this and me losing about twenty bucks playing nine-ball, they took me along to an underground club, something about how I wouldn't understand the black man until I could dance. They were laughing at me, not with me, but it was fun playing the fool. I felt a hell of a lot better after that.

Which all was smooth and normal until Sheldon and this crazy bastard. I shook that off for the most part. Practicing law has some weird aspects to it. It is considered a sign of racism if one is to think that all black people are criminals. The thing is, almost all the black people I come across actually are criminals. Most people I come across are criminals, period. After a while, the idea of people out there who live normal lives and manage not to commit or be indicted for felonies seems far-fetched, like some weird myth.

I was doing a bit of mental hygiene work at one point. A person would file a petition alleging that someone else was mentally ill and a danger to herself or others. Then there would be a small hearing to decide whether that person should be committed. Usually pretty clear. Guys would start talking to imaginary people in the corner, start ranting about how we were all tools of the Catholic Church, and so on. I was there to look after the interests of the person being committed.

I'd get a copy of the petition and an evaluation from the appointed psychologist before I met with the client. The latter would explain the problems, the evidence of illness, and so on. This time I had a middle aged lady, maybe forty. She was somewhat attractive, in a classic sort of way, a semi-statuesque black lady. She sat down and was telling me about how her husband was a liar and she was fine and so on while I was reading through the evaluation. It said "Claims to be a white woman locked in a black woman's body." Interesting.

So I brought it up. "Did you tell the psychologist you were a white woman trapped in a black woman's body?"

She looked at me, shocked, and forcefully told me "I never said that."

"Hmm. He wrote it down he...."

She cut me off. Looked me right in the eye, and flatly stated "I am White."

Well. I'd come to the belief by then that these sorts

of classifications were at the core arbitrary, so my first honest reaction was that she could be whatever the hell she wanted to be. No skin off my ass. "O.K."

She didn't let it go. "Are you telling me I'm not white?"

Which makes things weird. I mean, the lady has issues. I feel bad going along with her but I guess on some level I agree with her. She can be whatever the hell she wants to. "You say you're white, you're white."

"You don't believe I'm white."

"I believe you are what you say you are. It really doesn't matter to me." I tried to move on. "So, what kind of medi..."

"It matters to me!" She yelled. "People are always tryin' to tell me I'm black. There's some black guy out there telling people he's my husband. I ain't married to no black guy. I have WHITE babies. Forty of them. All white. With my real husband."

Hmm. "Who is that?"

"George Clooney."

"You living with him?" At this point I'm just trying to keep communicating, maybe find some fact she believes that I can tie back in to reality. I've seen a lot of lawyers just shut down the interview at the point it becomes clear that the client is completely delusional. I've found that doing that can start agitation and paranoia and make the hearing a total fiasco.

"He still loves me. When we're together he's so sweet to me and the babies. If other peoples around he acts like he don't know me. He got real mad once and got me thrown in jail."

"When was that."

"Back the time I's in LA trying to talk to him. I ain't seen him awhile and was scared he was gone. He snuck into the jail to visit me though. I guess he can't let nobody know we married 'cause it messes up his career, all those women wanting him."

I jumped off at that point. I commiserated with her a minute and explained how the hearing worked and popped out to get the bailiffs and the mental health judge. She was committed, of course, and sent off to a hospital to get her bipolar medication back on track. It was a rough hearing, watching her husband have to listen to all this stuff about her being white and the white babies and how he wasn't her husband and George Clooney and on and on.

Just awful.

IT SAYS HERE...

It didn't occur to me until later to ask her why it mattered if she were white or black. Hers would have probably been as good an answer as any.

XI) Doors

Criminal law is, if you think about it, all about doors. We hold ornate ceremonies using archaic concepts of human sensory reliability and scientific evidence that completely ignore the concept of double blind methodology, wherein twelve people largely chosen for their being unqualified decide whether a person gets to be able to open his door for maybe a day, or maybe the rest of his life.

They are some serious doors. Lawyers try to explain the difference between jail and prison many ways. The technical difference is that jail is where you go awaiting trial or if you manage to commit a misdemeanor and really piss someone off by being black, poor or having a victim who is or knows someone. It is classically run by the county sheriff or a city, but these days counties and cities sometimes pool resources to have regional jails. Prison is where felons go to serve sentences longer than one year.

So the clientele differs quite a bit.

To me the big difference is the doors. When you first are in a modern jail the doors seem loud. Usually all you are dealing with is the sally port, which is two big sliding doors, only one of which is open at a time. One opens, you go between the doors, the first slams shut, and the other hopefully then opens. In a regional jail the interview rooms are usually right inside there, and the doors to those are nothing special.

When the port doors slam shut, it makes all the noise a huge slab of steel makes. You can tell the new lawyers by the little involuntary jump. This goes away after ten or so trips.

That is, or one trip to a serious maximum security lockup. County lockups have candyass doors compared to a big prison. Thicker, grayer, and just heavier somehow. Before one of these open there is a sudden crack of some interior latch snapping open. The acoustics couldn't be harsher. This crack makes the slamming shut of the jail's port doors seem like the sigh of a baby kitten. Plus the doors are way thicker and completely solid. No windows like what make up most of the port doors.

The other big difference is the number of the damn things. In the regional it is just the port. In prison there is a door, another door, and some more, and maybe an elevator. Any of which couldn't be knocked down by a speeding truck. One trip in there and you now really know what it means to be inside. You will go nowhere unless someone hits a switch.

And that is just general population. Where it gets awful is when you go into segregation, jail inside of jail. The hole. This is even further away from daylight. You go in the room one way, through two extra hallways bracketed by huge doors. I used to think the doors at the courthouse holding cell were heavy after I tried to catch one with my shoulder and got knocked over. These are a whole different level. The guards usually needed quite a bit of force just to move these things. Seriously solid.

The client comes into the room from the other direction. If he is in segregation for something silly like selling drugs or refusing a cell mate the guards are pretty lax about the visit. If the client stabbed a guard, the guards are usually a bit more vigilant unless the lawyer once pissed them off, and then the lawyer is on his own.

I had one client that refused to visit except through the non-contact window with telephones thing. He told me that if we were in the same room and he were to get upset he'd attack me. "I've stopped trying to control myself," he explained. "Why bother? I'm not going anywhere unless you get me out." Nothing is more chilling than a total sociopath with keen insight.

I do admit that was one of those cases where the whole process of trying to get this guy out of jail was a bit conflicting.

While the guards escorting the prisoner stick around to watch the prisoner, the guard escorting me doesn't need to stick around to see if I try to escape or shank someone.

So once I've discussed what I can do to get someone who can't even manage to keep himself out of jail while already in prison back on the street, the guards on his side take him back to his home behind his personal door. Meanwhile I wait for someone to let me out. The prisoner escort says he will let my escort know to come get me.

These are the occasions where time stands on end. My watch is in the lockbox in the lobby. I am roughly twenty tons of steel away. Ten minutes go by like ten hours. There is a communication panel if I want to talk to Charlie

Brown's teacher. I usually don't. I've been stuck from ten minutes to two hours. Usually I have a book.

Except for the time the prison power plant went out. Of course I didn't know that at the time. All I knew was that I was in the dark, surrounded by concrete and steel. Doors so thick that if you scream and beat against them there is not even an illusion that anyone could possibly hear you. Trust me, I would know. Almost more flex in the walls than the door. In these days of electricity and streetlights we really don't know dark. This was dark.

Nothing there but me. Wanting the power to come on, having mixed feelings about someone getting the door open because for all I knew this was a riot. After a while, it got really weird. Weightlessness, times when what was inside my mind was more tangible than the floor.

I played eighteen holes of golf. I named all fifty states. I went over every case I had and thought about legal issues and scratched out brief notes that to my surprise could later be read. I relived episodes of youth, some happy memories but some not. I laughed out loud, and cried in the dark. I may have been asleep, but by the end I couldn't tell whether I was awake or not.

Later I found that I was in the dark for six hours.

Then the door opened and a guard came in, white as a sheet.

He was stuck in the hallway outside the room. We were maybe ten feet apart, and had no idea even though he claimed we had been pounding on the same door.

XII) Sexual Perversity in West Virginia

We were trying a sex case. Back then we were getting one big case each term, mainly child sex cases, serious stuff. On the books, sex offenses carry a certain term of years. In the real world, these crimes are charged in bunches which means that the wonder of consecutive sentencing allows a judge to hand down a life sentence.

Like the one time my guy was convicted of two hundred counts of buggering his son, while the kid was between six and fifteen months old. Yeah, I had a real good chance winning that one. Each of these carried a possible thirty year sentence. The psychological report, part of the pre-sentence investigation, said that someone should go back to everywhere this guy ever lived and start excavating the area looking for bodies.

The judge, surprise, wasn't really thrilled with this.

IT SAYS HERE...

The hearing was the type of sentencing hearing that makes me appreciate a good judge. I mean, I have to stand up and ask for probation or leniency or some shit. Pretty obvious I've no real argument to make.

A dickhead judge will sit there and act all shocked that you would suggest such a thing, and start fucking with you. A good judge will just cut you off, thank you, and move on. Either way, it is then time for your client to talk, which can be a train wreck.

In any sort of case involving violence, it is solid advice to not stand up at sentencing and rant about how the victim is a lying piece of shit. I once read one transcript where the defendant had been convicted of three counts of raping his estranged wife. He did nothing but complain to the judge about how she and his entire family lied about everything.

The judge thanked the defendant, and informed him that the order the judge had in his hands sentenced the defendant to three concurrent twenty year terms. However, after hearing the defendant speak, the Judge explained that he'd changed his mind, and that the defendant should never be free again, or at least until he is quite old. The judge wound up making the terms consecutive. In effect, the guy managed to talk himself into an extra forty years.

The guy in this case wasn't exactly helpful either, claiming that nothing he did with his son was anyone's business. I just cringed. The judge then sentenced him to thirty years on each count, all consecutive. Six thousand years. Only three thousand with good behavior and up for parole in two thousand, so it wasn't as bad as it sounds.

I wound up appealing on the ground that the state didn't prove two hundred distinct offenses and I threw in a challenge that the sentence was cruel and unusual. The appeals court told me to stick it on the first ground but agreed on the second and remanded for a new sentencing hearing.

The trial judge re-sentenced him to two hundred thirty year terms, all of the sentences but ten to run concurrently. In other words, three hundred years. One fifty with good behavior and possible parole after one hundred. Big difference.

At least the appeals court judges thought so. They affirmed the new sentence.

So even though the case we were now trying alleged fifteen hundred counts of rape, I knew my client was protected from having to serve more than six thousand years.

Somehow the guy was out on bond. The first day of trial was horrific. He was accused of raping his stepdaughter on a daily basis for years. The stepdaughter testified about it, her mother testified about catching them once, her brother about hearing it. The crowning glory was a tape where my client was discussing all this with the victim, including his statement that he "thought she enjoyed it."

Real close case. Beyond the evidence this guy looked like someone had asked central casting to send over a child-molester. He was old, but skinny with sharp features. He wore tight jeans, cowboy boots, and wore a dark blue jacket. His grayish hair was slicked back. The jury looked at him like they were deciding whether to convict him or just storm out of the box and beat him to death. Also a fun case. How do you cross-examine that kind of stuff?

"Are you sure it was your step-father that was the one raping you every day?"

So mainly I sat around feeling useless. At the end of the day the state rested. My client refused to testify. The trial was recessed for the day, and we were to come back in the morning for jury instruction and closing argument. The general consensus of those attorneys drinking in my office that afternoon, a group amounting to about two-thirds of the non-prosecuting attorneys in the county -- not much to do there and trials are like sporting events -- was that my client was going to run for it.

"No livin' way does that guy not know he's gone for good if he shows up. My guess is he's at least south of Memphis by now," was the way Bill put it.

So the next morning, having figured out what I can say at closing, I trudge into the courthouse. My client and his new family are there. The trial starts back up, we go through the jury instructions. I give a closing argument to a jury I can best describe as unreceptively hostile, an argument that uses the phrase "reasonable doubt" about fifty times.

The jury goes out. My client sits in the courtroom with his new family, all of whom seem rather confident or at least not worried. I figure the jury will be out for a while seeing that they have to decide on one hundred counts. The state dropped fourteen hundred counts at the end of trial to speed things up, which was nice of them.

The jury comes back in about three in the afternoon.

They are giving my client the death stare again, so not much drama. The judge asks the foreman if there is a verdict, gets the verdict form, reads the whole thing and goes through the whole thing and all that and announces that the jury finds the defendant guilty of all one hundred counts. I hear gasps from his family. My motion for bond pending sentencing is, believe it or not, denied.

So I'm sitting there collecting my papers and putting them into my satchel while the bailiff is leading my client out in chains. I hear his new family crying, mostly muffled sobbing.

Then one of them, a woman wailed out "Now who am I going to get to watch my daughter!?"

I can't make shit like that up. I heard it. The prosecutor heard it. Bill heard it. We were at the lawyer bar having a drink that evening. None of us mentioned it. It just sort of hung out there.

The next morning Bill was in my office waiting for me, wearing a look that could be described as confused and excited.

"Did you..."

I cut him off. "Yes."

"Watch my daughter!? Holy Shit!"

202

I shook my head. "How come we didn't talk about this last night at the bar?"

"Man... it was like I couldn't quite grasp it. It never really, you know, sunk in until I was driving in this morning. What the fuck was that about? After all that, she still wanted the guy as a babysitter? Seriously. What the fucking fuck?"

"Beats me."

XIII) "Getting what you pay for"

It may be a shocking fact, but there are some people who are wary of advice that comes from a public defender. Especially when those people don't like what they hear.

It happens quite a bit. Guy's guilty and gets an offer that is less than pleading guilty to all counts, but he's probably going to prison or jail anyway. I advise him that he's best off taking the thing. He's seen too many TV shows and complains that you aren't "fighting" for him.

I explain that we can go that route if he wants, but he's not likely to do much better than what they are offering. Actually, it is a near lock that he will do worse. A jury will probably look at the cruiser tape of his waving his dick at the cop and not really worry about the technical aspects of breathalizer calibration and just go ahead and figure he's drunk.

IT SAYS HERE...

Usually it ends with grudging acceptance. Sometimes they go for outside counsel, which can work out, don't get me wrong, but it can also be an utter fiasco.

I'm not dissing outside counsel in general. It's just that in these obvious cases most of the solid lawyers wind up echoing what I was saying. So the client looks until he finds someone who tells him what he wants to hear. Sometimes that lawyer is a maniac, sometimes he needs to pay the rent. I guess he could be onto something I couldn't grasp, but that hasn't happened quite yet.

DUI cases come close. In all but obvious cases money can buy expert testimony that destroys the credibility of the breathalizer. This goes about ten grand a pop. So us PDs don't get into this. If that is an option the case shouldn't ever pass through our hands in the first place.

There are stories upon stories of people suddenly finding assets they forgot to disclose on the Public Defender application and hiring "a real lawyer" only to wind up with the same obvious result or worse, and light a few grand to boot. Like the guy who waved his dick at the cops. An offer was on the table for him to plead to a felony 3rd offense DUI, and they would drop the companion felony for his 3rd offense for driving a vehicle while his license was suspended for DUI. A pretty generous offer all told, mostly because the prosecutor's office knew I'd have to try it unless I had a good deal and the Judge wouldn't care to hear it.

I figured we'd worked it all out until I got the letter from some lawyer in one of the bigger cities about 100 miles to the north. The lawyer was telling me that my client hired him and wanted me to send the file.

This is generally the best mail a public defender can get. Maybe once in a while you want to try a particular case, otherwise it is as painless a way to close a file as it gets. So off goes the file. Goodbye. Next case. I really thought nothing else of it. I figured if some other lawyer could get around the dick-waiving and talk a jury into acquitting the bugger, good for him.

An assistant prosecutor did mention the case to me one day. He'd got a phone call from the new lawyer wherein the lawyer basically badgered him about a better deal and how the charges were bullshit. The kind of behavior that just doesn't really work with a prosecutor. Usually this is for the benefit of the client, makes the client feel better about parting with a few thousand because this new lawyer is "really fighting for him" and so on. Apparently the new lawyer told this prosecutor that he wasn't as "slothful and ineffective" as I was.

This made the prosecutor burst into laughter. "I just laughed at him, and he hung up on me. I can't wait to see what this asshole does in court. I mean, he waived his dick at the cop. I'm tempted to take the deal off the table but I don't want to punish the poor bastard because his lawyer is an idiot."

As things worked out, I happened to be in the courtroom for some hearing or other the one day Judge Folsom happened to be running behind. This just didn't happen. Folsom was punctual to an absurd degree. He liked his trials fast, his hearings quick, and unlike a lot of rocket-docket types, Folsom would get orders out in a hurry. We had three terms of court each year, and in that small county the grand jury would meet once and hand down something like forty indictments. Folsom would have pretty much all his twenty cases resolved within the first three months. Usually there would be a straggler, some murder or molestation case or the like where a defendant had to be evaluated by a psychiatrist.. Other than that things flew.

I had no idea why Folsom was behind that day, but I

did know it had to give him a touch of the red-ass. Difficult to describe seeing Folsom was usually hangover cranky even though he didn't drink as far as anyone knew. Seeing I'm getting at all this it's pretty obvious that the hearing I'd stumbled across was the dick-waiver.

The new attorney was moving to dismiss the charges because, well, that's where it gets bizarre. From what I could tell he wanted them dismissed because the area he was pulled over wasn't exactly downtown, and therefore "nobody lives there."

Well, the first problem with this is that this isn't any kind of defense to drunk driving. The guy was on a road near the north border of Franklin County over on the other side of the Old River Gorge. It wasn't the main road, but he was maybe a half-mile away from the major north-south artery through the state, and for that matter through the whole region seeing there would be a lot of people from Canada and Pittsburgh and such going to Florida on that road.

In fact, the big bridge crossing the river just north of town was pretty famous for silly people jumping off it. Most of them would use a parachute and try to miss the rapids below, but there were those that skipped the parachute and could care less if they hit the water or the rocks. A few local cops liked the occasional suicide. They'd get to use the scuba gear and get some overtime.

So it wasn't exactly true, and it wasn't exactly a defense even if it were true. The fun part is that we've not yet gotten to the real reason this lawyer really, really fucked up.

You see, Judge Folsom was from up around there, which is bad enough, but it gets better. That big bridge over the gorge is somewhat new, maybe thirty years old. Before then it was a giant pain in the ass to get to that part of the county. If the county had been drawn up by someone with some local sense rather than probably some drunken idiot, that part of the county would have been in a different county on that side of the gorge.

The upshot of this geography lesson is that the main political power structure developed south of the gorge where most of the people and businesses were. So those living north of the gorge were for all purposes a minority with no real say.

"Nobodies," would be a way to put it.

Folsom had managed to get his (elected) post mostly by force of personality. He was a Judge down to his

DNA. He looked it, he talked it, and he probably even smelled of it. People liked him, unless they were criminal defendants, in which case they were probably headed to prison so who cares. He was largely immune to the typical bullshit inane party political nonsense that anyone else that wanted to hold an elected post had to wade through.

He did have a rather large chip on his shoulder when it came to where he was from and how his community would get shafted by those south of the gorge. When that out-of-town big(ger) city lawyer said nobody lived north of the bridge, well... Folsom levitated about an inch above his chair, his eyes lit up like a jack-o-lantern with a hundred watt bulb inside, and his bushy white beard seemed to stand on end and widen. It was impressive.

"Nobody lives up there, eh? Let's see. The first road off of the main road is Three Mile. The first house on the left belongs to Joe and Gene Bremmer. They bought it from the Harts, for whom I babysat in high school. The first house on the right..."

On he went about ten houses deep off every road off the highway all the way to the county line. Who lived there, for how long, and even a decent short biographical sketch. Very impressive. All the while looking the lawyer dead in the eyes and implicitly daring him to show the slightest bit of disinterest.

When Folsom finished, he asked the lawyer if he cared to clarify what exactly he meant by "nobody."

"Your honor, we withdraw the motion."

"Why? Did you not see those houses when you no doubt drove through there to carefully establish a good-faith factual basis for your claim that 'nobody' lives around there? Or are you admitting negligence when proffering facts to This Court?"

"Um..."

"It's quite simple counselor," Folsom boomed. "Either you admit negligence, for which I will find you in contempt, or you can pursue your claim that these people are "nobody" for which I will find you in contempt. One of these gets you forty-eight hours in the jail, the other a fine. Not picking gets you both."

"I apologize for my negligence your honor, I made an assertion of fact that was reckless and completely inappropriate hyperbole as well."

The lawyer wound up with a five-hundred dollar fine. Two weeks later it was a different lawyer entering an appearance. A month after that the defendant took the same

IT SAYS HERE...

plea offer he was offered in the first place.

XIV) Exit Strategy

After I left Franklin County I bounced around a bit. I didn't mean to but I pretty much got thrown out of the second county I practiced in. I had a dumb case. Some drunk eighteen year old kid was running around one night and stole a car. "Steal" is a bit loaded as he was clearly not planning on keeping the thing, and unless you plan to "permanently deprive" the owner of the car it isn't technically theft. With a car that's called "Joyriding."

So the kid is out Joyriding, and at some point he also took a wallet out of an unlocked parked car. That's theft. This kid wasn't likely to be featured in the local paper as the "Teen of The Week." Fair enough. He did it. He admits it. Should be simple from there, right? The kid pleads guilty to a misdemeanor or two, gets some probation, and life moves on.

Of course not.

First thing that happens is that the officer charges him with a felony. Overcharging is like a sport among some officers. Some do it to facilitate plea bargaining as it gives the state a position to move off of. Others do it because they are Barney Fife incarnate and felony cases make them feel important. Some are just mean. Others don't care all that much. Most of the time weak felony cases plead out to misdemeanors at the preliminary hearing. Sometimes against the wishes of the officer, but in those cases it has to be a really weak felony.

In this case the officer just didn't show up. So the case was dismissed. I warn my client that he can still very well be indicted for the felony or even charged with a misdemeanor for all this, but he officially right now has no charges pending. I close the file, and the kid winds up moving to North Dakota to live with his mother. I didn't know this at the time. I just closed the file and thought nothing of it.

About a year later, the kid winds up being indicted, but just for stealing the car. The indictment notice is published in the paper, andwe send a letter to the kid's last known address. The first thing that happens once a grand jury indicts someone is an arraignment hearing. This is when the guy that is being indicted is formally notified that he's being charged, and then a plea is entered and a trial date is set.

I hadn't heard anything from him, and he didn't show up. Happens. Technically, all they have to do is put a notice in the newspaper. If you don't show up, you are a fugitive. Doesn't really matter except if you get pulled over for speeding and the officer checks the computer, you get arrested as a fugitive from justice. If you are in another state this can be really weird.

This kid doesn't show up, the fugitive warrant is issued, the file goes back into storage until this kid pops up on the grid. That takes about two years. One day, out of the blue, I get a call from his panicked mother. The kid was living in Wyoming, and had tried to enlist in the Army. It appears as part of this the Army runs a candidate's identification through law enforcement computers to make sure there are no outstanding warrants or charges. Whoops. They find a two year old fugitive from justice felony warrant, the local heat is advised, and the kid winds up sitting in some jail in Hellknowswhere, Wyoming.

So I work the phones. I call the prosecutors, see if

they would be willing to just let him be, drop the charges and forget all this seeing it's a pretty silly case to begin with. I was dealing with one of the more reasonable assistants, who had hashed it out with his boss and so forth and they decided that Wyoming was just too damn far to extradite someone for a minor felony, but they just couldn't let it go.

What winds up happening then is that Wyoming lets the kid go, but he stays in the computer as a fugitive. It is just that Wyoming has been notified not to bother. The kid could still be picked up and put in jail if a particular officer didn't know about the not to bother part and so on. So the kid is in Wyoming. He calls me and I explain the situation. He's been a fugitive for years. West Virginia isn't going to have him sent back here unless he gets picked up in a neighboring state because they just don't care all that much. However, he's still a fugitive.

The kid wants to get this all straightened out. He wants to go into the military and not have to worry about getting arrested all the time. So I set up a date for him to appear in court to answer his indictment and the fugitive warrant. He rides the bus to West Virginia for the hearing. About five days worth of bus. We enter a plea of not guilty.

IT SAYS HERE...

We get a trial date about two months in advance. The fugitive warrant is lifted and my client is freed on his own recognizance, the judge figuring he's about the opposite of a fugitive at this point. Of course, once the kid gets back home he's going to have about thirty minutes before he has to get back on the bus, but so is life.

In the meantime, I'm trying to work out a deal. This should have happened quickly, but it doesn't. It is one of those things where I know something odd is going on. Anyone who looked in on this case from the outside wouldn't notice, but when you do case after case after case you get a feel for things. This case is one where the kid should plead to a misdemeanor. Problem is, there is no deal coming. What confirms the oddity is the behavior of the prosecutor. Nothing he can do about it. If there was a reason he could tell me, he'd tell me. But he's not giving any reason, so I know he's being forced. He knows that I know that he's being forced, and he also knows that I know he can't even tell me he's being forced. He also knows that I'd have to be dumber than a Marshall dropout not to figure out he's being forced for reasons he can't tell me.

You get the picture. The first time this happens between people trying to keep a congenial working relationship, there is a bit on non-verbal apologetic communication from the prosecutor., After two or three times any need for this goes away. We both know the score, he's being pressured.

It isn't too tricky to figure out what it is. Usually it means the victim is "someone" or that my client has really managed to piss "someone" off in the past. My guy has no real history here. I found the guy whose car was "stolen" and that guy could care less, says he did that sort of thing when he was young and figured this kid probably didn't need anything more than a fine if that. The victim went so far as to contact the prosecutor's office and request that the charges just be dropped. They weren't.

A bit of a mystery. Not one that I worried about. I prepared for trial. I liked the chances seeing there wasn't even a good argument that the kid was going to keep the car. Problem was, sometimes juries don't need good arguments. My client didn't love the idea of jail, but jail shouldn't be an issue no matter the verdict as long as he could pass a piss test. The big problem was being convicted of a felony. Those tend to restrict the opportunities a young person will have in life. Plus it takes away the right to vote, and probably more important to my general clientele, the right to possess a firearm, without which it is hard to hunt.

Three weeks before trial, the prosecutor still has no help as far as a deal goes, but we manage to get a continuance for some schedule contrivance. That particular judge tended to be backed up and any hint that there could be a possible deal would make him willing to continue the damn thing as much as we wanted. I figured the prosecutor was still trying to get something on his end, and my kid wasn't in a hurry. So it got bumped six months.

I was ready to try the thing, so I was just waiting.

Still waiting.

Two months later, I got a curious phone call. It was from a lawyer I'd seen around the courthouse; he did a bit of criminal work and we had defended co-defendants a few times. He was a bit of a political player, he did work with the legislature and had a connection or two, ran for prosecutor once, that sort of thing. He asked about this kid's case. Said he wanted to ask me off the record if I was going to get pissed off if he maybe tried to get some wheels going.

"No problem," I chuckled. "I don't even know where the wheels are much less where they got stuck."

"It's one of the victims. The guy who lost his

wallet."

"The empty wallet? The state didn't even bother to indict on that. Hell, the arrest reports don't mention the name, and the grand jury report doesn't even mention the wallet."

"Yeah. That's the problem. The wallet belonged to a guy who has some pull, but I know someone who knows someone and I was going to talk to that guy about it if you didn't mind."

"Feel free. Can't see how you can fuck up the deal I don't have working."

So I had to figure out who the hell the wallet belonged to and what the hell this had to do with anything seeing the charge had been dropped. In the movies I go get a trench coat, bribe some officer to get into a records room, and then find some wild piece of evidence that leads me to victory at trial against the forces of evil. So I'd get the trench coat, but the officers wouldn't let me in so I'd go to the bar and ask around.

I find out who it is. Big Wheel type rich guy. I kinda figured that. Once in the State Senate, and lost a few times trying to get into Congress. On some committees here and there, silent influence in the Democratic Party, the One

True Party in West Virginia politics. Did I mention that the prosecuting attorney and the judges are elected? No?

I'm guessing the Big Wheel didn't want his name in the reports. However, he wants the kid punished as to his wishes so he is giving the prosecutor heat about making any deals. Kid just picked the wrong wallet in the wrong neighborhood. Not much I can do about this, just wait out the silent power struggle and then go to trial.

The morning of trial finally arrives, my client is fresh from the Marathon Man bus trip. The prosecutor arrives with some vague plea offer that he says is probably going to be offered but something about victim notification about the car. I wasn't worried about the car owner. There are more hurried cell phone calls, and I'm just sitting there on a bench talking to my client about his trip.

After about ten minutes the situation clears. The Big Wheel had agreed to allow a plea to the joyriding if my client would also plead guilty to petit larceny for the wallet. Problem was, the car owner objected to the deal and said his preference was that the whole car deal be dropped, but this bothered the Big Wheel for some reason and then He got over it so the offer was a petit larceny. My client was willing to take the deal to avoid maybe getting a felony. So then we sit back on the bench and I explain the Constitution and such to the kid, while the prosecutors get into a mad scramble to get the paperwork needed to enter a plea.

Then we enter the plea. Sentencing set for six weeks later, after a pre-sentence report can be had. A pre-sentence report is when someone in the probation office writes up the recently convicted person's life story and gives the results of the all-important piss test. When it came out it showed that the kid had no criminal history. The kid had a bit of alcohol trouble, but since the arrest went through an inpatient program in North Dakota and had been clean since then. Just give the kid a fine and let him on his way back the hell out of town and into the Army. Kid's now got a record, and that should be enough.

Except there still is the Big Wheel. I tell the kid not to leave the stove on when he comes back for the sentencing.

So the hearing gets here. There is some guy with gray hair and an expensive but ill-fitting suit. I'm mildly surprised he's here. Usually political thug types just act behind the scenes. I figure he's there just to watch my kid get six months or something for no reason. I'm wrong as usual. The judge comes in, I give my spiel about his lack of criminal record, signs of his rehabilitation, that he's planning on joining the Army as soon as this is all done. The prosecutor basically mumbles with his eyes lowered that the state is asking for jail time because theft is still a crime and so on.

I will say it was refreshing, getting to see a prosecutor argue for an outcome without having any helpful facts. That's usually my job.

Then he says the victim would like to speak. I'm surprised. Then the guy stands up, makes sure the Judge knows exactly who he is, and then.... well... something like this.

"Your honor. I live over in the east hills in a quiet little neighborhood. My house is on Gildemar Lane, and it is a little dead-end street, more like a cul-de-sac with ten other houses, all nice, close-knit families. We are very happy there, but a few years ago this kid here changed our lives for the worse. My wallet was sitting in my car, a car I always left unlocked, and this kid just took it. Now, it didn't have any money in it or anything, but the sense of violation was overpowering. We never had problems like this before, no crime. After this we've been scared of what might happen.

I've had to put in a two thousand dollar alarm system. Every day now for over two years I have a new nighttime ritual. I actually go around the house and make sure every door is locked. I even go out to the car and makes sure the doors are locked. Now, late at night, whenever a dog barks, I start to wonder who might be out there and what he is doing.

I want this Court to consider the effect this crime has had on my family. I want him punished to pay for the fear he has given me and my family. Thank you."

I was trying to figure out if this was all a joke. The judge asked us to stand and he sentenced my client to six months in the county jail. No reasons, as usually are given. This marks the time exactly one week before my house was officially listed for sale. I fear I lost it.

The Judge asked if there were any other motions. Heh.

"Your honor, may I be found in contempt?"

"What?"

I sighed and stated in a very worn manner: "Well, Judge, what just happened here was the most ridiculous miscarriage of justice I've ever seen or heard about, at least not involving a Lindbergh, and I'm a bit worn out by the president of Candyland's moaning about being fed the apple from the tree of knowledge and not appreciating the painless lesson in reality my client gave him, as it could have been someone a bit more hard-core that could have found his unlocked door first. So I don't really want to jump up and down and scream, but unless I get found in contempt I don't think I can call myself a lawyer or look in the mirror."

The Judge stifled a grin. "Mr. Jobertski is found in contempt. Hundred dollar fine."

I was ready for that. I brought two one hundred dollar bills from my poker bankroll. "Can I approach the clerk to remit the fine?"

"Sure."

I walked over and slapped the hundred on the bar. I was unfortunately way to pissed off. I held up the second C-note. "For another hundred can I ask how the Court can sleep at night doing shit like this?"

Grin disappears. "That will cost you another hundred dollars and twenty-four hours in the Regional jail." Or words to that effect.

Now I'm grinning. "Thank you, Judge," I say in cheerful voice and manner. The Judge just left the bench.

The Bailiff tells me to wait at the table so he can go get another set of cuffs. I take off my jacket and tie and give them to another lawyer who witnessed the thing. I whip out the cell phone, and leave my wife a message that I'd be a bit late, would stay at so and so's house instead of making the drive tonight, and that yes, I agree that we need to move. Then I gave my phone, keys and wallet except for my driver's license and the twenty dollar jail fee to my pal, told him to pick me up at the regional tomorrow. That is if he could stop giggling by then.

I barely got through the booking process. We got to the jail, and I sat on a bench joking with the guards and my client, and becoming some sort of folk hero among the prisoners when they heard what had happened. Things moved very slowly. They finally booked me, and then since I was about six hours away from release they didn't bother to assign me to an overcrowded cell. I suggested they just park me in the jail library, and they did. So I sat in there reading a biography of Margaret Thatcher, of all things. Then they gave me back my stuff and I walked into the lobby where half the defense bar was waiting for me. Someone used that "heyyy...you broke your cherry" line from "GoodFellas" and I had to let the lot of them take me to dinner.

I wanted to sleep. Eventually I got my car back and drove home. I told my wife had what happened. I didn't have time to get into the story when I left the message, and that was a story that had to be told in whole. The bailiff would cut me some slack, but not that much...

Some wild ironies surrounded this whole deal. The Judge never pushed anything with the bar because he obviously didn't care to have to explain the sentence, and once he learned I was leaving he didn't care. He called me into the office for one of those "On the record, if you do anything like this again, I will have your balls cut off, off the record, I do about half-apologize for being a whore" type discussions. Since then, that Judge still assigns me to trouble cases even though I moved into another county.

That has something to do with the effects of my stay in jail. Going to jail does wonders for your reputation among people who are in jail, doubly so if you get there by "fighting for a client." This doesn't do you much good if you are looking for high-dollar work, or maybe it does. I've never looked and we don't have enough high-dollar criminal work to bother looking.

I moved to a bigger, urbanish county some distance

from that one, but it used the same regional jail. When some guy stuck in there would mention to a guard or anyone that he had me as an attorney, well, it was better than any letter of recommendation I could bring from my eighth-grade math teacher. I don't talk much about this anymore, but it's a lot of the reason I handle trouble cases well. The story gestated at that regional, and repeat business being what it is, spread enough through the system that if someone had me as a lawyer they'd hear about what had by then turned into the month I pulled on behalf of my client.

I can't explain why I did all of this. The Judge that started all of this accuses me of planning the whole thing, which isn't quite true. I just decided that if they sent this kid to jail, I was a complete wimp unless I got myself tossed in as well. I was so scared when I did what I did that I was probably even money to pass out. I was angry, but this just wasn't in my nature. I forced myself to overreact. I figure I maybe was afraid of doing something wrong so I just went and aggressively did as wrong as I could and took the consequences. The rest just fell into place.

XV) Well... at least I have that.

At one point I fled trial practice and was hiding out in post-conviction hell. I did appeals, petitions for writs of habeas corpus, so mainly I'd write extensive detailed well researched petitions which I hoped someone would at least read before they were turned down. West Virginia didn't have an appeal of right back then, the one appellate court could pick and choose what cases they felt like hearing. It may shock the gentle reader to hear that they shied away from serious awful type felonies with obvious reversible error. Did I mention these people were elected?

So that was a big help.

Worse was the habeas nonsense. After the appeals court refused to hear the case, the convicted guy could petition a normal trial-type court. Thing is, the petition usually went to the court where he had his trial in the first place. Good luck getting that same judge to suddenly decide he made the wrong decision before and the murderer or rapist or whatever should be tried again like five to ten years later.

Plus, the habeas stuff had no fixed time limit. There was some weird law where the guy could keep filing petitions until he was appointed counsel who would then file a petition that made some sort of sense. As long as the court kept tossing the petitions without appointing counsel, the guy could file another petition. This could go on for years.

Like the Price case. Guy is convicted for "felony murder" thirty years before I saw the file. People sometimes see the term "felony murder" and think that it is some sort of super bad awful variety of murder. It isn't. Usually it is quite the opposite.

Regular murder requires someone to kill someone else with malice aforethought, meaning you thought about it and meant to do it on purpose, more or less. Felony murder is a bit different. It means someone was killed while the accused was committing a felony, mostly old-school items like robbery, rape, or burglary. Although West

Virginia tossed in drug dealing as well, not that it has anything to do with this story.

This whole idea came about back in England a few hundred years ago. Back then, if you committed any felony it was your ass anyway, so if someone got killed they called it murder. Only practical difference was what they said you did before they swung you from a rope. The idea stuck though. If you mean to commit a felony and someone dies by accident, the intent "transfers" and as far as the law is concerned you meant to kill that someone. Ergo, you are now a murderer. Sorry about your luck.

This sticks because prosecutors claim it makes it easier to prove a murder and put bad guys away. Don't worry about us misusing it, they say, we would never do that. Trust us. We won't use it more against some people because they happen to be poor or whatever.

Price was poor. Although his problem was more in the direction that his victim happened to be someone's mother, more specifically a state senator's mother. Nothing like politics to ensure an even-handed response from a prosecutor.

Back at the time Price was a young punk. During his Senior year of High School one thing led to another and he and another person decided to break into a house. Price didn't really know the guy, didn't really think much about it. They waited until the cars were gone and the lights out.

They pried open the door. Price looked around the downstairs collecting shiny things he figured he could sell. The other guy was upstairs looking for stuff, or so Price thought. What the other guy also did was find an old lady sleeping soundly in her bed. He took a pillow, and covered the lady's face, pressing down until he felt her stop struggling. The other guy also found some cash and a radio.

Price and his cohort split the stuff and the cash. Price hid his half of the stuff, figuring he could pawn them in a few weeks. He had no idea what had gone on upstairs. He took the cash and got stupid drunk at the bar.

The next morning, he was awakened by his mother, telling him the police were there wanting to talk to him. Price staggered to the door, andthe officer asked him if he'd broken in to the Lewis house down on the corner last night. He told him things would be OK if Price just told him all about it.

Price figured they had him. So he told the truth, told them who he was with, told him where he hid his half of the stuff. One can only imagine the confusion on the part of the officer until he realized that Price really had no idea that someone was killed. One can, however, imagine Price's bewilderment when he was arrested and charged with first degree murder.

West Virginia still had the death penalty back then; this was before the United States Supreme Court hit the reset button on the death penalty back in the early seventies, the court requiring a bunch of procedural safeguards before a state could legally whack someone. Price didn't know that would happen, and neither did his lawyer. So the deal where the prosecutor would promise to recommend life if he plead guilty seemed like a good idea. Still up to the judge, but seeing it was undisputed that Price not only had no part in the killing, but also didn't even know it happened, it seemed unlikely that a Judge would sentence him to death.

So he entered the plea. Legally he was dead in the water as to fighting the murder charge. Best he could hope for was a life sentence and parole eligibility in ten years.

Meanwhile, the Senator had a few words with the prosecutor, and probably the Judge, but maybe not. At the sentencing hearing, the prosecutor violated the deal and asked the judge to kill Price. He put several witnesses on the stand, relatives of the victim who cried, told stories about the victim, and begged the judge to sentence Price to death.

So the Judge did. The other guy never made it that far, having killed himself in his jail cell. At least that was the story as far as anyone cared to ask.

Price's attorney's appealed. During the process the death penalty was abolished and Price's sentence was changed to life in prison without the possibility of parole. It took two years for his conviction to be overturned on appeal, even though the prosecution's violation of the plea bargain was plainly obvious.

So Price was back to square one, but there were no deals on the table. His choice was to plead guilty and have a judge decide if he should ever be eligible for parole, or to go to trial and have a jury decide. Given the political reality, the choice was obvious.

His new counsel did what he could at trial, which was not much. The whole trial really wasn't about guilt or innocence, it was about whether Price would ever be eligible for parole. The way it worked then, and still works now for that matter is that the jury just decides whether the defendant deserves "mercy." No guidelines, no standards, the jury just decides on a whim. If there is mercy, he gets a chance at parole after ten years. If no mercy, he stays for good.

The jury found him guilty and gave him no mercy. His appeal from that conviction was denied, and he then started the long trail of habeas proceedings. He filed eleven that were denied out of hand, and then the for the twelfth he was appointed counsel. That was also denied by the circuit court, but on appeal the West Virginia Supreme Court sent it back to the circuit court for no clear reason. That was where I wound up inheriting the case when I made the leap into post-conviction work.

The original habeas corpus petition mostly dealt with the claim that the jury was tampered with. A few stray witnesses that said that someone else said that the bailiff told the jury that the defendant had also molested some kids, but the evidence couldn't be used at trial. One of those things that seemed a little too specific to be a complete lie. The bailiff was dead by now, and none of the jurors that were still alive cared to talk about it. So the circuit court dumped the idea for lack of proof. Once there is a conviction the whole "presumption of innocence" stuff goes out the window, and the defendant has the burden to prove any claims he has about the trial being improper.

A cynical person might tie that in with the first eleven petitions being tossed with no real comment. That maybe twenty years after the second trial, after the bailiff was dead, counsel being appointed to help so that an evidentiary hearing could be held was not coincidence. Most people who are demented enough to take on a pure post-conviction caseload tend to be a tad cynical.

The first thing you have to do once you get one of these cases is to read the record. Given the history of this one the record was a bit big. Also a bit old. One hint for those thinking about working these kinds of old cases: don't do it if you have allergies to mold or dust. Paper ages when it sits in boxes, thousands of pages filling ten or so bankers' boxes doing nothing but sitting in the corner of various offices. Boxes of notes taken by the, as far as I could tell, twelve lawyers that handled the case before me. I was the lucky thirteenth.

Post-conviction work is for the most part an exercise in futility. If there was some really good issue to be argued usually the trial lawyer would keep the case. Having post-conviction specialists available presents a difficult choice for a trial attorney. An appeal is a lot of work. On the other hand, giving the case to someone else means that other person is going to read the transcript, and that very thought fills the heart of many a lawyer with dread. Having everything you say over the course of a trial memorialized in print is bad enough, but someone else reading it and looking for problems is for many a harrowing prospect.

When a case goes through more than ten hands, it isn't because none of them wanted to touch the wonderful issues inside. Usually each attorney finds no decent issues and is looking for a reason not to have to do anything final. That or the client is completely insane and demands the attorney raise some issue that either makes no sense as to law or has no basis whatsoever in fact.

There are some decent jailhouse lawyers out there, but there are way more that have no clue what they are doing. What goes on with these guys is that they mentally can accept no conclusion other than the one that gets them out of jail, and that makes things weird. Usually the trials putting these guys in jail weren't exactly close.

It is like Sherlock Holmes in reverse. That whole "Once you exclude all impossible conclusions, whatever remains, however improbable, is yadda yadda." Except for these guys it is more like once you exclude all possibilities that confirm guilt, what is left, no matter how outlandish, is what really happens or is how the law really works or whatever. Most of these guys aren't stupid, and they apply a great bit of energy, intelligence, and creativity to develop these self-serving analyses of law and fact.

At first there is a perverse pleasure in trying to make some sense out of the fifty page memorandum sent by one of these guys. Eventually you figure out that there is no sense, that their biggest tool is uncertainty in the face of overwhelming and precise adverse data. So they confuse the issue, even to themselves. Rookies visit the jail, discuss it for a few hours, and leave with the impression that progress has been made, only to be surprised to be confronted with the original arguments again. The emotional investment is staggering.

So I get to go through the whole record, just in case everyone else missed something. Of course, that assumes everyone else actually read the fucker, so maybe I'm being a tad excessive about just how futile it feels. Digging through boxes of yellow paper, trying to find the fatal flaw in some quarter century old trial. The judge is dead. The defense lawyer is now a federal judge. Hell, the guy you are trying to save isn't really the same guy that was tossed in jail. Thirty years of the routine. GED classes, doing various jobs, sitting in jail with no real hope of ever knowing anything else turned him from a punk to an outwardly polite person who learned the lesson that behaving on the inside resulted in him getting privileges, and that was a bunch better than being tossed in the hole.

He was, as odd as it seems, married. Maybe not so odd. Much has been written about women that marry prisoners, something to do with control and such. Who knows. What I do know is that she's a pain in the ass, and she seems more desperate for him to get out than he is. That was the thing about Price that made his case bearable. He wasn't the lawyer type and wasn't demanding the presentment of weird legal theories.

There is no dramatic way to describe the process of discovering a huge error in a trial record. You just go through the whole thing and now and then it just occurs to you that something is unusual or that maybe you should investigate a certain detail just in case. Ideas come to you in your sleep, while driving to work, and so on.

I had read the whole damn thing and had some ideas that fell flat. One weird thing about the trial was that the state presented and had identified as exhibits the autopsy photos of the victim. The state didn't oppose the defense argument that the pictures were gruesome and not admissible as evidence. So they were not entered into evidence.

This whole thing was rattling around in my brain when I was golfing one afternoon. Just playing by myself, getting some exercise by carrying my bag. I was in a bunker after blasting onto the green. I tossed my club towards my bag and as it was flying through the air everything seemed to freeze.

It was creepy. The club just hung there as it shot through my mind that the Judge had sent all the exhibits back to the jury, which meant that the jury had the pictures of the autopsy which were never entered into evidence, and thus the record conclusively showed that the Judge himself had the jury consider items that were not legally evidence during their deliberations. Which was as basic an error as error gets. You can't have juries deciding cases based on things that aren't evidence because that just isn't a trial governed by the rule of law.

Then the club hit the ground.

I wasn't sure that the judge really sent the autopsy

photos back to the jury right then, but I wasted no time picking up and race-walking to my car to go back to the office and check and make sure. I fumbled my way through the door, grabbed the last volume of the transcript and started near the end looking for the part where the judge sent back the exhibits to the jury.

Yep. He sent them all back. We were in business.

That, however, was the easy part. The hard part was getting something done about it. I wrote the petition and filed it, getting a hearing date two months later. Nothing to do but wait.

A month later my phone rang. I picked it up, and the receptionist told me my wife was on line three. I pressed the button and said "Hello, honey!"

"Excuse me? This is Judge Martins. Is this Elbow Jobertski?"

I made a mental note to thank the receptionist for getting me into this jackpot. "Sorry sir, little mix up there."

"Good. I was worried about you there for a second. I got your petition, and..." He went into a five minute speech about the importance of a habeas petition in a life-without-mercy case, how it was the prisoner's last chance for relief, that given West Virginia's lack of an appeal of right it carried extra weight here, and so on. It was more or less the exact same speech I had heard from another judge up north a week or so before. I figured I knew at least one of the subjects that came up during the last judicial conference. "...So I would like you to know that the Supreme Court has sent the case back down to re-examine the file and submit a new brief,"

"Sir, I filed a new brief last month. Do you mean another one after that?"

"Did you send me a copy?"

"Yes sir. I've a time-stamped copy here in my hands right now if you would like another."

"Oh. Never mind about all that then. Just send that over." He hung up the phone. Judge Martins could act strangely sometimes, which made things interesting. Interesting isn't always a good thing though.

I had talked to Price about this.. He could have cared less about getting his conviction overturned. He wouldn't have minded all that much, but what was closer to his heart was getting parole eligibility. I figured Judge Martins' sudden interest marked a good time to maybe open some negotiations with the prosecutor's office about making a deal. I figured the law required the conviction to be reversed, but it wasn't that simple.

First of all, Martins was fully capable of just flatly denying the petition, which would leave me at the tender mercies of the State Supreme Court. They were very capable of just ignoring it. Even if Martins dropped the conviction and ordered a new trial, who knows what rulings he would make about using transcripts on re-trial. He could also decide that the conviction was just fine since Price was obviously guilty, but that the mercy determination needed to be done over. Any weird rulings could eventually be raised in a habeas petition in federal court, but Price wouldn't have counsel and federal habeas rules are notorious for their rigid time and procedure rules. File something wrong or not in time and you are barred for good and sorry to make you cry.

So it would be best to just make a deal and get parole eligibility. Hopefully the prosecutor's office would not want to get into a lottery with Judge Martins that could result in the whole conviction being tossed.

Eventually all that happened. The judge showed signs of dumping the conviction and the deal was made. Price went from no hope to on the track to freedom. He was transferred from the maximum security human warehouse to a medium security joint where he started his battles with the parole board. From my end the big difference was that his wife stopped bugging me about the petition and hearing and started bugging me about the parole board.

At that point it was out of my hands. He finally did get out. Sometimes when I wonder whether or not my whole career is some sort of sick joke, all this time spent researching and writing briefs, defending the indefensible, and all of that, I think of Price. The stupid kid that was going to be killed for his poor choice in crime partner, who wound up spending his whole adult life in prison having no reason to believe he wouldn't die there until for some odd reason the door opened and out he walked into real life, reborn at fifty, all for deciding to burgle a house he believed empty.

That is always the one thing I can point to, late at night when the Doubt Fairy pays me a visit to make me consider whether I'm worth a shit at all.

XVI) Yes, there is the occasional unpleasantness.

Usually it is a completely reasoned response. I've never snapped at a client out of a loss of control. I will admit I will do it out of a strategic need. One of the many pitfalls of being a public defender is that your clients don't pay. For some reason people who don't pay for something are far less reasonable than those who do. So often I wind up with a less than bright individual who will often change his story in mid sentence while at least once every five minutes whining that you (a) aren't following him, (b) aren't trying to help him, and/or (c) are working with the state. He's also convinced that, not only is he smarter than you, but so is every random jackass he talks to in jail.

There is no reasoning with this guy. He just lacks respect for you, and anything you do will just make him act like more of a dick. This leaves you with one move. Get in his face, yell at him. Makes him think you care, and makes him hesitant to be a jackass just to do it. You just went from being some sort of flunky to being a real person.

Sort of the same effect as if he were paying you. There is a cost for jacking around, so he usually quits.

Of course, every now and then he will just attack you. Which clears things up as well as you just got off the case. Plus that makes a great story. One tip is to always put the client closer to the wall, so if he starts up you can pin him to the wall with the table.

Then there are the cases of Total Rage. Everyone gets mad, even completely monkey-tilt crazy over something, but most people can calm the fuck down. Most people. Others can't. One case was a guy that had been in prison for about six years for what was admittedly pretty small potatoes for a life sentence; just that he caught a prosecutor that didn't like him so he got the business end of the three strikes law. There had been a mild amount of prosecutorial misconduct, nothing jaw dropping goofy or anything. The guy was clearly guilty, nobody could really dispute that. Dropping off your live-in girlfriend at junior high is not a good fact to have come out in a statutory rape case.

However, the guy was always pissed off about all of this. Always. Shaking angry mad. I figured it was just when I was around, he would get mad thinking about the case. Other inmates straightened me out. As the saying goes, he had an even disposition: he was mad all the time.

Sometimes a client will get fed up to the point where he complains to the state bar. I've come to love getting mail from the state bar disciplinary board. At first it is scary, but once you realize you have your shit together to a reasonable degree, and that a lot of your clients that file these things are, well, nuts, the comic effect comes through. Usually I'm not required to respond to a client's allegations because they are facially absurd.

Sometimes I am, but the response isn't tricky. Like the time I was accused of general ineffectiveness as pertains to a trial that took place three years before I graduated law school, and in a county I still have yet to visit. That was a quick response.

Longer responses can get a bit trickier. One guy accused me of telling him to lie in court, which I have to admit isn't a totally unreasonable claim, an incorrect claim, but understandable given the complexity of the situation. What had happened is that this guy wound up being

247

convicted of a mess of child molestation charges, but he maintained his innocence.

The law here is that if you are convicted of a sex crime and want to be considered for probation rather than prison you have to have what we call a "sex offender" evaluation. The catch is that your guilt is now assumed as a matter of law, so if you continue to maintain innocence you are considered to be in denial or refusing to accept responsibility. This is then in turn an indicator that you are likely to be a pedophile, and that finding would inspire the judge to hammer the person at sentencing.

So, the obvious advice is to pass on the evaluation unless you can admit to the crime. Otherwise, you are just giving the court extra reason to hammer you. Since you likely aren't getting probation for a ton of molestation counts, your only hope to again be free is that the judge doesn't run all the sentences end to end so that the total minimum sentence is longer than any reasonable life expectancy. A finding by a psychologist that you are an incurable pedophile with no sense of remorse isn't good for this.

What often happens in reality is that the client still maintains innocence, but doesn't want to give up on the chance for parole. So what happens is that I have to, gently, suggest that if he did in fact do it, it would be a really good idea to just come clean with the psychologist because otherwise the evaluation is likely to be a nightmare. I then have to continually explain I don't want him to lie to the psychologist, but seriously, if he did it he's best off if he just says so.

This conversation usually goes in circles, and in this case he decided I was trying to set him up and reported me to the bar. Thankfully the bar understood my explanation.

Alright, back to the weird things.

One mundane, but strange one was a client claiming I wasn't in contact with him and wouldn't visit him but I wouldn't say why. To support that, he included with his diatribe copies of the six letters I sent him explaining that I was still collecting the record and until I had it I had no reason to visit.

That one, as you might expect, was tossed without me having to respond.

The one that really hit the mark as to strangeness and underlying symbolic weirdness was when I was accused of being a prosecutor. No, not in general in some sort of sense that I was working for the state, I was accused of being a specific Franklin County prosecutor acting as a defense counsel under an assumed name.

Which was weird, because that prosecutor and I had a lot in common. We were from the same area up north, we both went to the same college, albeit not at the same time as he was twenty years older, and both married girls from the same town with the same first name. We had similar builds, both played hockey, and had similar, although pathetic, FIDE chess ratings.

So we joked about that here or there. Well, until some wit at the bar decided to not just kick out the complaint and made me answer it.

Which was annoying, but fun in a way when I had to tell people that knew us both that yes, I needed a sworn statement that we were two different people. I was hoping for an actual hearing. I like to think I'd have had the prosecutor stay home and when he was to testify I'd put on a fake mustache and pretend I was him.

I wouldn't have though. Maybe.

Anyway, enough of the bar complaint business.

Some clients are just weirdly irrational. One guy was on trial for a felony, third offense driving while his license was revoked for DUI. Also known in the biz as

SRO/DUI (Suspended or Revoked Operator's for Driving Under the Influence). He was also charged with a few misdemeanors having to do with illegal car equipment.

How he got picked up is a story in itself. Some cop is in a rural spot running his radar, probably hoping he doesn't catch anyone, when one of those pickup trucks with really big wheels comes ambling by. Problem is, there are flames shooting out of the bottom of the thing. So the cop decides to stop him before the thing explodes. On go the lights and siren, and the truck pulls over.

My client comes stumbling out of the driver's side and face plants on the road. Out of the passenger side flies out some guy that was maybe three feet tall. He did a neat barrel roll, stood up, and started puking before he realized he was on fire. Then he did the stop drop and roll thing.

The poor cop didn't know whether to check on the prone driver in the road or the flaming midget. He dragged my guy out of the road and went to the little guy who was sitting on the ground laughing hysterically because his vomit had caught on fire. He was, obviously, shithoused.

Turns out my guy was sober, and the other guy not driving, so all they had on my guy was the no license charge and some spare change having to do with the truck.

The offer from the state was to plead guilty to the third offense SRO/DUI and everything else would be dropped. Given my guy was driving and they had a bunch of paperwork showing he'd been busted not three times, but seven times for the SRO/DUI. A no-chance case if there ever was one.

However, the guy was convinced he spotted a technicality. In some of the paperwork the officers described the offense as "DUI 3rd" instead of "DUI/SRO 3rd." This was completely meaningless as the indictment, the actual charging document, got the thing right and accused him of SRO/DUI 3rd. Explaining this took some finesse, as it turned out.

"Those arrest reports don't matter. All that matters is what is in the indictment."

"Bullshit!! These reports were filed in the court file!! That makes them official."

"No, that isn't so. It just means they were turned over to me by the state."

"Are you working for me or them? I'm no moron, those are filed so they are official!!!"

This went in circles for a while until I thought of a new angle. "I can file anything, it doesn't make it official, it just means it is in the file."

"No fucking way."

So, I took out my legal pad, ripped off a sheet, and drew a big smiley-face. Under the picture I put the words: "See!!! I can file anything!!!!"

I then told him, "I can file this. If you want me to, I can come back tomorrow with a copy with the official stamp and everything."

"No, you can't."

I just shrugged and left the jail. The next day I went to the circuit clerk to file the thing.

"I've something unusual to file." I handed over the paper to the clerk.

"Good Lord, Elbow. What is this about."

"Long story. Some guy thinks everything in the court file is the word of God or something, and in his interests, not to mention the county and the ten grand or so a trial would cost, I need to disabuse him of this."

She just shook her head and stamped the thing and my copy for my client. I took it back to the jail. He laughed when he saw it, and then decided to listen to me and took the plea. Probably saved him all in all seven months of jail, and saved the county probably twenty grand all told. I still want my cut.

Still, this was nowhere near the worst, or for that matter, the weirdest case.

That one stands alone. Guy is awaiting trial for a number of felonies based on his keeping an ex-girlfriend hostage over a period of months and beating her and raping her repeatedly. There was a big missing persons report, face on the news and so on when she disappeared. At some point the family mentioned the ex-boyfriend to the cops, that he was a bit of a loose cannon, so the cops went to ask him about it.

Sure, this doesn't say much for the family or the police that it took months to bring up the asshole ex-boyfriend to the cops, but that is a different story.

When the cops knocked on the door, the boyfriend panicked and drug the girl out the back of the house and was caught trying to drag her away. The girl gave some statements, a medical examination confirmed that someone had been beating her and raping her repeatedly, the family now suddenly remembered some threats he had made, and so on.

Believe it or not, the guy did not get along with his first few attorneys. So I wind up with the case, read the file, and go to the jail. It was a rather interesting conversation.

They wheel him in. My college courses in anatomy pay off because I know he has one leg fewer than normal. I introduce myself, he refuses to shake my hand saying something about "cocksucking lawyers," and I ask him how the jail has been treating him. Small talk, try to calm him down, don't come on to heavy. He is silent for a while.

"SHE'S A FUCKING WHORE!!!" This is the maddest I've seen someone in my whole life, before or since. Veins bulging, eyes popping out, and he's bouncing a bit in his wheelchair.

"Okay. I assume we are talking about Jane?"

"YES!!! SHE'S A FUCKING WHORE!"

"So what happened?"

"SHE'S A FUCKING WHORE!!!"

"Okay, I understand that. Can you tell me what was going on?"

"SHE'S A FUCKING WHORE!"

"Right. Do you mean you paid her to stay at your house?"

He breathed in violently and shook his head. He started to say something and gave it that grimacing pause. He continued, somewhat more softly but with a totally tense jaw movement, sort of through clenched teeth but a bit more animated. "You didn't see her whoring around when she was with me. She is a fucking whore." He spit the last words out, bobbing his head.

"What do you mean she was with you. Was she staying with you or something?"

He looked at me like I was the dumbest person on earth. "I had her there because..." he then went back into rage mode "SHE'S A FUCKING WHORE!"

I just looked at him for a second. "I don't really get it. Are you saying you were keeping her there because you were worried about her moral character?"

"SHE'S A FUCKING WHORE!"

"So you are saying she's a whore?"

Okay, that was probably uncalled for, but I couldn't really help it. In a weird twist of irony it appeared that was what he wanted to hear. So he nodded wildly and went on a maniacal monologue.

"That bitch has been whoring around ever since she left me. She fucked Greg from the gas station, our landlord, and three other guys I don't even know. She was out all night drinking and partying with a bunch of niggers!!! She was probably fucking niggers!"

IT SAYS HERE...

Racism is a common issue when you represent poor white rural people. Their problems aren't so much interpersonal issues as much as racism being roughly the same thing as to their moral compass as water is to a fish's physical world. It is just there, intrinsic to reality. They often get along fine with blacks. They do get worked up over interracial relations, and I've been told more than once that the bible says that it is wrong for the races to mix by people that are otherwise reasonable and even socially liberal. I am the guy's lawyer, so I'm pretty much forced to just be neutral. My usual policy is to just murmur sympathetically. Back to the rant.

"She wasn't doing that when she was with me, was she? I want the landlord called as a witness. I want Greg called as a witness. SHE'S A FUCKING WHORE!"

I shrugged. "I don't think that is an defense for holding a woman in your house against her will though, if you are saying that is why you did it. We really need to discuss this beyond your opinion of Jane."

"BUT SHE'S A FUCKING WHORE!!!"

I figured I would just ask some questions. "They say you were dragging her down the alley. How did that happen with you in a chair?"

Deep breath. He then replied as if distracted a bit. "I had a fake leg."

"The jail took your fake leg? Why?"

"I tried to beat someone with it and then threatened the guard."

"Okay."

"Plus she's like half-paralyzed, she can't use her right side."

"Right."

The switch flipped again. "AND SHE'S A FUCKING WHORE!!!!"

"I see."

It kind of went downhill from there. I wound up having to withdraw from the case because of rather specific threats of violence he made regarding the alleged victim and the female lead prosecutor involving using both the water pitcher at counsel table and, believe it or not, his wheelchair, even though he was handcuffed to it.

"I've been practicing." He explained. "I can hop on my leg and swing it around pretty good. I'm gonna nail that bitch."

A defense attorney has the right to disclose information to prevent a future violent crime, and I tend to consider it a moral duty to do so even if there isn't a legal duty. First, I explain clearly to the client who makes a threat that I understand he's just blowing off steam, but he can't tell me about some future crime he plans on committing because I have to disclose the threat to prevent physical harm.

Usually it really is just blowing off steam. That or the client takes the hint and just doesn't tell me about it anymore.

Not this dude. "I'm not kidding. I'm going to nail the bitch. Don't worry, I'm pretty sure I'll miss you."

So I warned him again, he again convinced me of his sincerity, so I got to wash my hands of the matter.

XVIII) The "do it yourself" drug culture.

Addiction and stupidity are a recipe for absurd tragic comedy.

When I started in this racket Oxycotnin and other pain pills were the real big drug problem that would end the world. Lots of prescription fraud cases, many of which were kinda hilarious. Mostly what people would do is take a legitimate prescription and change a number, like some doctor was really going to write a script for "600" pills over thirty days. With the last zero in a different color from the first two numbers. Maybe cross out the number of pills or the dosage.

Pharmacies became a popular burglary target for a while until security measures were beefed up. Then I helped have a pharmacist busted for shorting people on prescriptions when he blamed a client of mine. Towards the end of the first wave pills were going for about twenty bucks each depending on the dosage. The media screamed from on high that the end was near. All of a sudden being addicted to painkillers wasn't strictly the sport of the rich.

Then it sort of petered out, at least if you judged by the papers. What really happened is that prescription drug abuse just became part of the criminal law landscape. It mostly came up when someone would get busted committing some crime to get pills. Beyond prescription forgery there would be straight up forgery, using stolen credit cards, mostly paper type crimes. The person would get busted, usually confess immediately, and plead guilty for a recommendation of probation for a first offense. About half the time the person would take this seriously, get help, and quit being a mess. The other half would bounce back into court on a probation violation, get back out with a requirement of inpatient treatment, and usually get kicked out and wind up in prison for forging a fifty dollar check or something.

There was a weird justification by a lot of these folks that the actual stealing or forging wasn't wrong as they were stealing or forging so as to pay the rent, get groceries, or even to pay child support.

Of course, this was because they had already spent all their money on the addiction. What really struck me as ironic was that all too often what the forged check or stolen credit card was used for was to buy cigarettes. Layers of addiction.

The irony was that this made things safer. The "hillbilly heroin" made the real heroin all but vanish from the local drug scene. Heroin is a lot harder to get from raw materials to the street. It involves a pretty coordinated enterprise, smuggling, and so on. So it is more expensive than the pills, and, well, anyone that would rather have a heroin ring in their town than a couple of script forgers, pharmacy burglars, and the occasional doctor free with his prescription pad is a fucking lunatic.

I'd like to think that this was part of a reasoned policy response to the drug problem, but I'm not a moron.

It was just a natural result of massive drug interdiction efforts. Those make it hard to move things around that usually need to be moved quite a ways from source to user, like coke and heroin. So the response is to shorten the supply lines, as it were. The pills only became contraband once they were unauthorized, and that would generally very close to if not actually in the possession of the end user. In short, the risk of transportation made moving stuff so expensive that the demand shifted to local goods. Simple economics.

Unfortunately, there are those who view the reality of drugs as a simple evil rather than a fact of life subject to supply and demand, as is any other commodity. If people don't want it, it goes away. Thing is, people want it, and they want it a lot. Why? I don't know. Life sucks, self-medicating for depression, boredom, or maybe flipping pancakes at IHOP is a little more interesting stoned. This is a culture where we have massive amounts of people addicted to caffeine and nicotine and think nothing of it. Just have a drink and relax and so on. People sometimes like to feel other than how they feel right now, and a drug is the quickest path. Normal human behavior.

So we shroud most of it in ignorance and give it a seductive quality that only forbidding it can achieve and we have widespread addiction, not to mention dumbasses snorting VCR cleaner. Meanwhile we cut down supply, and the poor who are most vulnerable to chemical escapism have to pay huge prices and who stole my car?

Enough of that. What all this economic babble leads

us to is methamphetamine. The beauty of meth is that the raw materials are everywhere. There is nothing that has to be brought in from Columbia or Afghanistan or wherever. That cuts off a bunch of the distribution problem.

So at first we have professional-type laboratories ran by wayward chemistry majors. People that understand the chemical process. Materials are bought in bulk, the lab is set up in a rented house, and the meth is cooked. The cooks then take the meth and leave the mess. Nasty mess. Less distribution means the meth is a much less expensive stimulant than crack, so it becomes popular. More labs.

Eventually it gets big enough where media outlets can start screaming about a new "epidemic" that will make everyone crazy and shoot your dog for no reason whatsoever. Cops figure out what the raw materials are and a general effort to control mass sales ensue. The feds start sting operations against the biggest players and are very effective.

Problem is, it doesn't take much stuff to make meth, and the recipe isn't extremely complicated. Plus there are still as shitload of people still hooked on the stuff. So smaller labs pop up, which are eventually busted and so on.

At some point in here is where the labs start

popping up in West Virginia. By probably not much of a coincidence this is when amateur hour begins and some complete morons get into the game. People that wouldn't know a hydroxyl group from a bluegrass group. People start setting themselves on fire.

Making meth isn't that hard. The difference between a pseudoephedrine molecule and a meth-amphetamine molecule isn't much. Just what is called an hydroxyl group, more or less a single atom of hydrogen and a single atom of oxygen. You may be aware that two atoms of hydrogen and one of oxygen make up water. So what you need to do is hit that hydroxyl group with an atom of hydrogen. The way you do that is find something with an extra hydrogen atom. Which is what we call acid. Not LSD, but real chemistry-type acid, which is basically stuff with an extra hydrogen atom which looks for things to fuck with, which is how acid dissolves things. More or less.

So to make meth you knock that molecule off and then clean the stuff up so it doesn't burn a hole through your head. It isn't completely that simple, but how this is done exactly is something I'm not about to put into print, but it's no tougher than making a souffle'. The process isn't that difficult to understand but to do it safely and effectively requires some attention to stoichiometry, a fancy way of saying you need to pay attention to amounts. If you act like a bachelor cook and measure ingredients by precise measures like "too much," "some," and "just a little bit," then things will not go well.

So I start getting these cases. Mostly silly cases.

The first one of note was the Fischer case. Learned several lessons from that one. It was like going to Meth Harvard. Fischer was a sort of hippie leftover, except a bit too pissed off to be a real hippie. Then again, I guess any hippie that lived through Reagan and into the Dubya years can't be faulted for being a bit testy.

Fischer knew what he was doing. Problem was, the cops knew what he was doing as well, so they tried their best to get him. The best they could do was one of the most bizarre and weakest cases I've ever seen.

It all started with a theft complaint. A total bullshit theft complaint. One thing you need to make meth is a bunch of matchboxes. Not the matches so much as the striker plates which are a source of red phosphorous. So he wanders into a convenience store and buys all he can carry. Yes, he had a receipt the point of sale computer confirmed he bought a bunch of matches. No matter, the store filed a shoplifting complaint with a picture from the security camera of him walking out the door. With a bunch of matches. In one of the store's shopping bags. Not to mention they had pictures of him paying for the matches...

How it started I don't know, but it appears in retrospect something that the police realized could be useful. An arrest warrant for Fischer for shoplifting was something they could just carry around until they felt like serving it, arrest him, and search his car and person "incident to the arrest." It amounted to a free shot at a search without a search warrant.

So they did. Pulled him over one day and arrested him. They towed his car to the station and did an inventory search. They found a bunch of receipts for various materials used in making meth, like cold pills, drain cleaner, matchboxes and so on. Including one for the allegedly stolen matchbooks. In the trunk they found a bunch of empty Mountain Dew bottles and a black bag.

Mountain Dew is the lifeblood of the meth world. It is hard to find a cook or user that drinks anything else, and the bottles usually turn up in the homemade labs. In the black bag was a slew of dildos, vibrators, a light bulb, and a piece of rubber tubing.

Didn't seem like much, but the cops decided it was enough to book him on a meth lab charge. A magistrate decided the tubing and the receipt was enough for probable cause and the case went to the grand jury, who handed down an indictment.

It is important to note the that the meth lab law in West Virginia is extremely broad. Or at least the way the prosecutors read the thing, a position with which the courts later agreed, was extremely broad. What it boils down to is if you have in your possession items used in the making of methamphetamine, and have the intent to make methamphetamine, you are guilty of operating a methamphetamine laboratory. The statute as read seems to require some sort of specific step at "operating or attempting to operate" the lab, but the courts decided that just wanting to sufficed as an "attempt," never mind hundreds of years of case law to the contrary.

So I wound up having to go to trial over a light bulb, some tubes, and a receipt. I really had no case over the complete bullshit shoplifting complaint as far as Fischer's defense went. Someone at the store needed a false police report rap, and shame on the officers that sat in court and with a straight face claimed it all seemed reasonable.

IT SAYS HERE...

The defense was kind of obvious. The light bulb and tubing was something used to smoke meth, not to make it, and while Fischer was in the jail he told me that there would be some white residue in the pipe. I had an independent lab test some of the stuff and it came back positive as meth. So in reality they had a few receipts, and some empty mountain dew bottles in a car Fischer was driving, a car that wasn't even registered to him.

Fischer was, of course, a meth cook. Not a big time one, probably one of the smaller cooks that knew what he was doing. He wasn't cooking that day, though, nor had he plans to do so in the near future. It all just seemed absurd. The state's case was that the light bulb and tubing was the meth making materials needed under the statute, and that the receipts somehow went to his intent to make meth.

That was the opening, anyway. The prosecutor kept making references to "this epidemic" and I'd object and the Judge would sustain it. Then the prosecutor did it again, and I'd object and move for a mistrial due to prosecutorial misconduct. The objection would be sustained but the remedy denied.

Then I'd get up and point out that we could prove the tubes and light bulb had nothing to do with making meth, and these receipts and such meant nothing, that this case was groundless and so on.

The state called the arresting officer. He testified as to pulling over the car, but didn't mention the shoplifting stuff. Then he testified as to the stuff in the car, the bottles, the dildos, and the light bulb and tubing. Then she asked about the receipts.

My first bright idea. "Objection. There is no foundation as to the authenticity of this receipt, that it is in fact involves a transaction by my client or that it reflects the items purchased." Solid objection, it seems to me.

The Judge wasted no time. "Overruled." Uh oh. Looks like a long day on the railroad.

So the officers got all that in, the receipts were in evidence as were the bottles. The arresting officers didn't know shit about making meth, so I had to deal with an "expert" from the State Police.

I was ready for that. My client was an expert at making the stuff, so between him, literature I managed to get from law enforcement meth conferences, and some dandy shady websites I knew a bunch about making meth. It got to the unfortunate point where at night I'd dream I was making the stuff.

He got up and went through his spiel. I was just bursting to know how the fuck an "expert" would hook the light bulb into the meth process. It was a tube connected to a light bulb with the bottom metal part removed. In it's place was a cap with two holes one hole had a receptacle, the other a tube about eighteen inches long. The meth was put in the receptacle while the user drew in on the tube. It was a sort of meth bong. Fischer claimed it was his original idea, which I believed because it made no sense.

I figured the expert was going to call it a "gas generator," which would be bullshit. Towards the end of the process one winds up with pure methamphetamine oil. This could be injected, but HIV being what it is, and given all the nasty shit involved in the process, virtually nobody is going to jam that into a vein. So the meth oil is turned into a meth salt, that whitish crap that can be smoked or snorted. The way that is done is by bubbling hydrochloric acid through the meth oil, which makes the whitish stuff appear.

If you look closely at any pills you take, the scientific name for the stuff is often followed by "HCl." What that stands for is hydrochloric acid. Most solid medications are the salt form of a substance. You make hydrochloric acid gas by mixing rock salt with sulfuric acid, found in some drain cleaners. That bubbles into the oil, and meth appears..

Thing is, a light bulb is way too small and brittle, not to mention the little receptacle makes no sense. It just doesn't work that way. Usually people use a mountain dew bottle. Using a light bulb is absurd. One thing it does do is make my expert less useful, as it being a gas generator could result in some meth salt forming in the tube.

Good Lord, he just said that Mountain Dew was popular among meth cooks.

"Objection. There is no found-"

"Overruled." Ye gads.

He finishes, pointing out all the uses of the items listed on the receipt, how they fit into the larger picture, and mostly trying to sound smart. He makes a point of mentioning that meth salt could form in the tube. My turn.

"Let me get this straight, you are saying this light bulb was used as a gas generator?"

"Yes."

"The purpose of a gas generator is to bubble gas through a pretty thick liquid, right?"

"Yes, it is used in the salting out..." and on he went through the process. Cops like to see how many times they can say things.

"So there would have to be some pressure built up in that chamber to get that gas out of the tube, right?"

"I guess."

"And according to you that can happen in a light bulb without breaking it?"

"I guess."

I sighed. "Have you ever tried it? Making a gas generator out of a light bulb?"

"No."

"That's because you have never in your life actually made methamphetamine, the closest you have ever came was that training in DC where someone made it, using real standard laboratory equipment, while you watched, right."

"I've had other training as well..." He went through his life's story. I did a sort of cross my arms, tap my foot and look at the ceiling combo."

"That's nice, now could you answer the question, have you personally ever made methamphetamine?"

"No."

"So if I ask you the volume, that is the amount of gas needed to salt out a batch of methamphetamine you would not know, would you?

"No."

"So when you are saying the bulb can be a gas generator, you are speculating, are you not?

"I base my opinion on my five years experience and training..." His life story again.

"Experience and training that does not include making meth, correct."

"Yes."

"Thank You. No further questions for this witness."

From there the prosecutor tries to make him sound smart and I just ask him about his real world experience.

Then the state rests.

I call a Chemistry teacher from Central High and get her accepted as an expert witness. I ask her what would happen if I were to put rock salt and sulfuric acid into a light bulb, then attempt to harness the gas through a tube to pass the gas through a thick liquid?

"The bulb would explode."

"How do you know that."

"I tried it six times at your request. The bulb exploded each time."

"Thank you." I turned to the prosecutor. "Your witness."

"Did you test this particular bulb?"

"We tested six of the exact make and model."

"Yes, but did you test this particular bulb?"

"No, I did not."

"No further questions."

The Judge looked at me. "Re-direct?"

"Just one question, your honor." I couldn't believe the prosecutor went down that line. It probably didn't merit a response, but. I'd prepared for it. "How do you know you didn't test this particular bulb?"

The teacher smiled. "Because it is still in one piece."

I sat down. The prosecutor didn't bother to ask any more questions.

The defendant always has the last say as to testifying. I advised him to not testify seeing as I had a nagging fear that the Judge would let the prosecutor get away with asking anything during cross-examination, like if he had ever in his life made methamphetamine or maybe said a dirty word. He agreed with me. So we rested.

I wanted the jury to be instructed that since the offense was operating or attempting to operate a laboratory, there had to be some kind of actual operation, some step toward actually making something. This was swiftly denied.

So the prosecutor got up and gave a closing argument that the light bulb was equipment and that the receipts showed he was intending to make meth, that the, ye gads, Mountain Dew bottles were common meth lab components as well, and that Mountain Dew was a popular drink among those involved with methamphetamine.

I had to get up and straighten things out.

"First of all, this light bulb just isn't a gas generator. The only evidence of this is the testimony of a man that admits he's never even seen or operated one. Meanwhile, you heard the testimony of someone that tells you it just isn't possible. Why? She tried it. It will not work. What is it? It doesn't matter. There just is no proof this has anything to do with the production of methamphetamine.

That, believe it or not, is the strength of the state's case. After that we have some receipts, found on the floor of the car and some silly story about Mountain Dew bottles. All of this in a car not owned by or registered to Mr. Fischer.

The law requires that there be something commonly used in the making of methamphetamine, and there just isn't anything here, unless you would like to convict a man of a felony based on the brand of soft drink bottles in the trunk of the car he is driving.

The state has come nowhere near proving beyond a reasonable doubt that Mr. Fischer was operating or attempting to operate a methamphetamine laboratory. Therefore you must return a verdict of 'not guilty.'"

The prosecutor got back up and just went in a holding pattern. She gave up on the light bulb and started screaming about how the bottles were often used in the process and that was enough. These bottles weren't carved up like they needed to be or anything. Just empty bottles in a trunk.

He was, of course, convicted. The next day the papers talked about how Fischer was convicted of operating a mobile methamphetamine laboratory.

It seemed to me, and still does for that matter, that whether methamphetamine fucks up your sense of reality more than reading and worrying about the horrible methamphetamine epidemic is a toss-up. One group of people have paranoid delusions about supermarket discount cards being used by the government to track their movements, while the other consider driving around with some empty Mountain Dew bottles, a few receipts and a light bulb "operating or attempting to operate a methamphetamine laboratory." You tell me which is further in orbit.

I guess one lesson to take away from all of this is if you become some sort of meth cook, switch to Mello Yello.

Fischer was quite the guru, though. I would spend hours with him at the jail going over police training materials and transcript testimony. We'd go through the way cops made meth and he'd point out all the things they did completely wrong. The cop way skipped some details that would keep from killing yield, and used some methods that increased the likelihood of a nasty explosion. Which was ironic, in that Fischer claimed that quite a few meth cooks had materials like this, and trusting them over their own hand-me-down recipes obtained from whoknowswhere, used the cop recipe and blew themselves up. The problem was not in the recipe itself, as much as it was the materials. The cops made meth in a laboratory with real equipment. The cooks were out in the wild with, well, Mountain Dew bottles and whatever else they could scrounge up.

I'd take his theories and work through the

stoichiometry of the process, call people I knew with knowledge and expertise in organic chemistry, and generally figure out that Fischer was completely right about everything. I wound up knowing more about it than probably anyone else in the justice system, but a fat lot good it did me in a world where Mountain Dew bottles were enough to convict.

Another insight into the meth culture Fischer gave me was that cooking meth is just as addicting in its own was as using meth. Cooking meth was in context a godlike act, the meth cook possessed a sort of redneck philosopher's stone. A cook would take a bunch of random household crap and turn it into gold, or at least a substance that those in the cook's world would value the same. Money would be lavished on the cook, and in absence of that all sorts of favors and promises would be offered. The successful meth cook held a tremendous amount of power, and power in any form is a tough drug to kick.

Fischer was trying to get the jail to let him set up a "Meth Cooker's Anonymous" program. He was pretty open that he had a problem with it, that he figured he'd get busted but he just couldn't stop. He also figured he could help some other people out that maybe didn't realize that cooking meth was addictive. The jail didn't ignore him, seeing that ridicule, however negative, at least qualifies as a reaction.

So, even though Fischer was sidelined for a few years, the methamphetamine scene rolled on.

The cooks were getting dumber and dumber. The sort of dumb that only comes from not realizing you don't know what you're doing. Cooking meth involves several different chemical reactions, and in many of these there needed to be some level of precision. That was issue one. Issue two was that there developed a faulty feedback loop between smokers and cookers. Smokers began to talk about how the meth "tasted," identifying a few taste components that their conventional wisdom assumed represented a stronger batch of meth. In reality, pure meth had none of these tastes, they were a result of errors in the process allowing impurities to get in the final product. Considering what the items used to make meth are, like drain cleaner and matchbox striker plates, "impurities" takes on a whole new meaning.

As a result, smokers liked the less pure meth, and in response the "recipes" that would go around were getting worse and worse, making the "taste" stronger and stronger.

After some time, much of the product that would be sent to the state crime lab when a meth lab was busted wouldn't even test positive for methamphetamine. It was just goo.

As time went on, I had a lot of cases that were just garbage. Literally. They would get a tip of a meth lab in a house, get the resident to agree to a search, and find a bunch of garbage bags full of meth lab refuse. Solvent containers, matchboxes, empty pill packages, the whole spectrum. No evidence a lab was ever operated at the house, just a bunch of garbage. Nothing resembling lab equipment either, just garbage.

What was going on was the development of a market for meth garbage. By that time the public was very well aware of the signs of a meth lab. Empty match boxes, bottles of solvent, empty pill boxes, that sort of thing. Cooks started to figure out that putting this stuff in the trash wasn't a smart thing to do. So they would keep it in bags in the basement or under the crib or wherever. Eventually they would run out of space. A popular solution was to offer free meth to their less affluent customers in exchange for the customer also agreeing to take a bag or six of the garbage.

The key flaw to this system was somewhat obvious: if the customer were busted the first thing the customer would do is try to roll on the cook. Broke meth-heads aren't the people to look to for honesty and loyalty. However, cooks were used to bartering their wares for services of all kinds. Pretty much everything but housecleaning, judging from the usual crime scene photos. Plus the cooks would often play offense by giving up a garbage mule in exchange for leniency or just to make it look like they cared, on the poorly thought out notion that dropping a dime on a mule would deflect suspicion from them.

The irony was that the cops never believed the garbage mule's story. There was more than enough to get a conviction, so they'd arrest the guy, from there the County Prosecutor's "no tolerance" policy would kick in, and the guy would run out of reasons to roll. A jury wouldn't care, in part because all they would have to find would be that there was any before-the-fact agreement for the mule to take the garbage.

The whole thing was a mess. I was in a sort of urban area when this stuff was at its worst, but I somehow had this reputation for handling difficult clients so now and then I'd get a case from a rural county where they ran out of attorneys, having to take one after another off the case because the lawyer couldn't remotely effectively work with the client. Someone had to be the last one, and I often was that someone. It helped a bit that a judge would usually tell the client that if I said we couldn't get along, that meant the client has waived representation and would be on his own.

Brummond was a strange example. One thing I quickly figured out is that sometimes these so called trouble clients have legitimate beefs with their attorneys. Brummond was one of these guys. He was up on meth lab charges, but had a defense that was a bit technical and required some knowledge of how meth can be made. In his case, I was the first attorney assigned to him that understood he wasn't spouting gibberish and nonsense. He had a point.

Basically, he was a guy that was selling counterfeit meth making materials to meth cooks. His master stroke was that he'd buy boxes and boxes of that cold medicine that was made of that crap that was useless for making meth. Using a scanner and laser printer he made fake labels by copying the back of a blister pack of the real stuff. He'd then glue that label onto the crap pills and sell them. He did similar things with other materials, like iodine, for lesser profit.

So basically he was selling completely legal items

with no intent of meth being made, so there wasn't a crime. Well, maybe fraud, but I doubt any prosecutor would have the gall to sell that to a jury. "Convict this man because he rips off and foils meth cooks!" Right.

All of the evidence should have been suppressed anyway. The search warrant was total and complete nonsense. The way the case started was that the cops found a cache of meth stuff in the woods just outside of town. These cops really didn't like Brummond, in part because they suspected he was cooking meth, but probably more because he was a registered sex offender and, well, could be a bit of an asshole.

The sex offender stuff was largely nonsense. In his youth, at nineteen, he had a fourteen-year-old girlfriend. He didn't even fuck her; he was just busted for feeling her up a bit, which wasn't even a felony and at the time just got him a five hundred dollar fine. However, a decade and a half later when the registry fad reached West Virginia, it was a sex offense involving a minor. So onto the registry he went alongside all manner of hard core perverts.

He was considered a bit of an asshole, but in a mildly respectful way. For one thing, when on home confinement for some petty bullshit, he managed to link the bracelet to his cell phone so he could go anywhere. You see, the way those bracelets work, or at least worked then, was that they were linked by transmitter to your home phone, which had to be a land line. That way, it was impossible for someone to wander too far away. Supposedly it was impossible to somehow transfer the link to a cell phone, but Brummond did it and got away with it until one of the local cops ran into him waiting in line to go to a movie in a town about one hundred miles away. They were impressed to a degree, but pissed in that he wouldn't tell them how he managed to do it.

He was a petty crook and semi-legal hustler, mostly because he didn't give a shit and didn't feel like trying to get straight work because he was tired of trying to explain that he wasn't a rapist.

Anyway, the cops decided to ask for a search warrant for Brummond's house on the ground that this pile of meth materials was "near" his house. This isn't exactly a strong link in and of itself, but the magistrate went along with it. They searched his house and found all this stuff he claimed to be counterfeit. He said that to the searching officers, the arresting officers, the magistrate at his initial appearance, the magistrate during his preliminary hearing, the judge during a bond hearing, and again at his arraignment. He told every attorney he was assigned. Nobody seemed to care.

Another thing he would tell them was that the allegation that the pile of meth stuff was "near his house" was utter bullshit. Again, crickets. He tells me this, so I go out there, and find that "near" was so wrong as to boggle the mind. He didn't live in the town proper, rather in a collection of about fifty houses on smallish lots a bit down the road from downtown. His house was on one end, and the meth pile was on the other end, plus one hundred yards into the woods.

So, that wasn't exactly a hard motion to draft. I just printed out one of those internet satellite maps and circled things, then pointed out that "near" doesn't apply to a house about a half mile away when there are fifty houses closer.

Fine. At this point I just want to see the meth stuff, maybe see if there are any false backs on the pills, maybe have an expert test the other stuff to see if it is pure, and so on. I call the prosecutor, tell him I want to take a peek to get an idea of what I want tested. He tells me the officer will bring the stuff to the hearing on the motion. All fine and good.

The county where all this was happening was, and probably still is, a basket case. For example, the officer that was for a spell the lead investigator on Brummond's case wound up on home confinement as a condition of bail after his arrest on sex charges. He was supervising the county home confinement program, and developed the bad habit of demanding sexual favors from people on home confinement. This ended pretty quickly, the officer was a fat lazy fuck, and shitkicking redneck women do not tend to be submissive. So one of these gals kicked the ever loving shit out of this officer, and the whole story wound up coming out as a result.

Another example is that they lacked the funds to have the deputies go on patrol. At an earlier hearing I'm sitting in the courtroom, wondering why there are about five deputies sitting in there as well. They don't seem to have any stake in these hearings, and for the most part were just laughing, telling alarming stories of police brutality amongst themselves. I asked the prosecutor about this, meaning mainly whether he knew the deputies were a pile of violence hungry geeks, but he seemed to think I was more curious about why they were there and told me about the budget crunch.

The main town was a small place, small enough that my first time through I assumed it was just a few abandoned buildings by the side of the road and passed it by. The day of the suppression hearing I had a younger lawyer with me, in part this was for him to help me and for him to get experience, but also I figured if my defense pissed off these gas and violence hungry cops maybe they would think two bodies would be harder to hide. I couldn't find a parking spot in the lot, so I had to park on the street. The other lawyer tells me he's going to take care of the parking meter. Fair enough.

I gather my files and then see him staring at the meter, a quarter in his hand and a bemused look on his face.

"Fucker won't take a quarter!"

"What?"

"Most it will take is a dime."

I checked the car and my pockets. "I don't have any change."

"Fuck me. Am I going to have to go into a store and ask for change for a fucking quarter?"

"Welcome to the big leagues," I grinned. "Be polite. We don't want these people to think we're big city lawyers coming into town trying to impress people by flashing around big currency or anything."

"I just hope she doesn't tell me I have to buy something."

The hearing went mostly as expected except the officer didn't bring the meth making materials. On the stand he more or less admitted that there were all those houses, but argued that a half-mile isn't that long in the scheme of things, which is true, I guess, if you're an astronomer or something. He claimed to have all the meth stuff in his custody. All fine and good; the judge said he would issue an order in the next week or two. So I made another appointment to look at the meth stuff.

The motion was, of course, denied, based on the legal principle known in some circles as "The Dirty Bastard Rule." That is just a semi-snappy way of saying that an unsympathetic client isn't likely to get many breaks. Or any breaks. Or basic fairness for that matter. If you look guilty near and across town can become the same thing in a hurry.

None of this wound up mattering though, because nobody ever found the damn evidence. All those meth materials up and disappeared somewhere. They didn't just tell me this of course, rather I had to make a trip or two up there to meet someone who didn't quite make the meeting.

Then I guess they got their stories straight and sent me a letter that the evidence was in the local state police detachment evidence room and had been accidentally discarded when the new head of the detachment ordered the evidence room straightened out. Of course, the date they gave for this was before the day of the hearing, the one where that deputy claimed he had all the stuff in his custody.

So what the hell was really going on I don't know. The city, county, and state heat all had a finger in the case. The town guys made the initial arrest. Or I should say that town cop that got busted did. He said he put the evidence in the state police locker but didn't log it in. The county geeks took over from there, and apparently didn't bother to grab the evidence, or even confirm it existed.

I mean, it doesn't take a genius to figure this out. No cop would be dumb enough to accidentally toss a big pile of meth making materials, logged or not. Granted, the more rural state police detachments tend to be staffed with people that get kicked out of the decent parts of the state for being incompetent, but they aren't completely useless. This was in the middle of the great meth scare. Every cop knew what to look for, they all had been trained to the gills as to what could be used to make meth. A cop tossing a mess of meth materials, logged or not, is about as plausible as a cop tossing a pound of cocaine. Even the dumbest cop is going to maybe ask a question or two.

So yeah, the pervert city cop sold the shit.

Nobody seemed to want to acknowledge that this was likely, which makes one wonder. The local prosecutor had the balls to oppose my motion to dismiss because, you know, they didn't have any fucking evidence. He wanted to proceed with pictures. However, between the vanishing and the cop lying about having the stuff in his custody, I think the judge had enough and flushed the whole thing.

XVIII) Colleen

The sky is gray, no big surprise in late November here, but it goes far deeper than that. My office building was the victim of a rather lame arson attempt. The building stands but my second floor office has been rendered inhabitable by the soot. A thin layer of gray covers everything. The files, which on the whole were already matters of gray in the sense that they were rarely black or white, and even less rarely mirthful, are now literally gray. I, often rendered gray by handling of these cases, became gray from handling the files. The office is likewise now literally as well as symbolically gray. The air is even heavy and gray.

A close law school friend, in fact the first friend I

made at law school, killed herself last night. I heard about it as I was trying to make some sense of the grayness that was my life's work. The rest of myself joined my hands in becoming gray. The first thing that happened during law school orientation was a mass gathering in the huge mock courtroom, where professors and the dean made speeches, some meant to assure, others to intimidate. For some reason they handed out the scholarships there, not so much the money as a little certificate. I was awarded a full tuition scholarship from the state bar association. I didn't know what to think about that first impression. I felt like a bulls-eye.

Immediately upon the close of the whole deal, as people walked out, she accosted me. I hadn't seen her before in my life, mind you, but she informed me that she was my friend now, that she figured she needed all the help she could get. She did this in a completely honest way but in good humor. The only way to fairly describe her was that she was quite strange. We don't have a whole lot of radically liberal California lesbians in West Virginia, and she added to that with being possibly the most quirky person I'd ever met. This made her by default someone I liked to hang around with. I've always had strange friends.

Plus, I don't think I could have avoided it if I tried. It did make me feel a lot better about that spotlight.

She was right that she needed help. Her first attempt at legal writing read like a mystery novel. She was, however, a quick study, and rapidly grasped why legal writing wasn't supposed to be suspenseful. It went from there well past my tutelage, not to mention my ability, until she won several awards for her writing her second year. We were never really close friends after that, but the first year of law school, while not life and death, is an intense experience that binds those that work together to get through it.

We'd have lunch here or there. She wasn't exactly well liked in general; she could be amazingly rude and uncouth to everyone except me. She would be rather open about things to where it made people uncomfortable. Nobody knew she was gay until she started showing people a picture of her girlfriend, and that went over like a lead balloon here. She wielded her liberalism with all the subtlety of an ax, and that also made people nervous.

We lost track of each other after law school until by coincidence I sought a position in the same office she was working in. She saw to it that I was offered the position.

IT SAYS HERE...

She left a year later for greener pastures but I'm there to this day. We saw each other here and there at the State Supreme Court. She was on the other side of the appellate aisle, a state of affairs I didn't think could last, but it did for three years. At the end she was in a bit of trouble for wanting to confess error more often than would be politically prudent. Liberal to the end.

So I have no office, a professional refugee, and I sit here at home with a gray box full of a transcript I need to read. I tried to wipe it off, to clean the box, but the gray won't come out, and it smells of a scent that I'll never be able to describe as other than gray. Inside there is a story, I'm sure a gray and tragic one, that led to three dead bodies. My lungs burn of soot and the nasty cleaning chemicals. My hands are now gray. Every now and then I as I sit here writing this, I cough up more gray. I am gray to my core.

295

XIX) All defendants are innocent; all lawyers are guilty.

It is, of course, all my fault whenever someone winds up in prison. For example, if you are on probation and have a positive drug screen or two you are likely to at least wind up in front of a judge, but stand a decent chance of staying out. But if you take off and wind up on the run for a year or two, you don't.

It is, of course, therefore my fault when the end result is a prison sentence. I should have maybe mentioned that running off from a court hearing is a bad idea. Then I was totally incompetent in failing to make the judge understand why a person who has a bunch of dirty drug screens and who takes off and leaves the state at the first sign of trouble is someone that should be left on probation.

The sad thing is that once in a blue moon I do keep someone like this out of jail. Sometimes there are some really good facts that can persuade certain judges to try a shot at home incarceration. One time the guy disappeared for a while and was arrested. They found him taking care of his Alzheimer's addled mother. He hadn't turned himself in out of fear his brother would have to quit his job and take care of her.

That is about what it takes, but those I deal with are not exactly into nuance. Since someone they hear of didn't go to jail, the only thing keeping them from staying out is that the lawyer must suck.

Trial work is all your fault, all the time. Trials I can handle, it's the probation, parole, and home confinement hearings that will kill you. Just not a damn thing you can really do about them. If the probation officer doesn't want the guy back, he goes to jail. Appeals work is more of a slow depression. Everything is pretty fucked up already and you are just not usually able to fix things. People don't get into jail on your watch; they just don't get out, which is mildly more pleasant. What gets to you is they almost never manage to get out, even when they should.

I decided to get out of my second stint at trial work about the same time I had four trials in one week. One of those perfect storm deals. Plus all four clients were in jail, which made things real fucking convenient. So I'd do a trial, wait for the jury to convict and make sure I had a family member to bring the next guy clothes. If not, I'd hopefully have his sizes on file and clothes that fit in the office's clothes drawer.

If not, that afternoon I'd wind up going to a store before going out to the jail to wait for the guards to find the guy so I could talk to him. Waiting for the third guy was a fun time. The guards told me he wasn't in jail anymore. That only took a few hours to straighten out.

Losing all four didn't help, although the cases were all more or less hopeless, but unfortunately not completely hopeless. So much effort would go into finding angles and arguments and problems with the evidence. Then watch the prosecutors just screw up enough to give some hope.

Then the jury would convict, evidence that they weren't retarded and that I was probably losing my sense of objectivity. When you start out with a hopeless case and make any headway you start to believe that just maybe...

...But after the verdict comes back it brings with it a bit more reality. How could they convict? Yeah... that whole confession and eye-witness thing.

The general failure of nerve that led to my move came well before this streak. I just didn't care for the way day to day business was done there. Which probably led to the streak of trials because I more or less stopped trying to convince clients who were claiming wildly unlikely innocence to maybe consider a deal. Innocent? Let's go to trial.

Some of the deals offered bordered on the offensive. The best was one that offered to let my client plead guilty to the sole count of the indictment, with no sentencing recommendation, but he had to help the state by rolling on his co-defendant.

If you are keeping score at home, this is worse than just going into court and pleading guilty without a deal.

It isn't like I really cared if they didn't want to offer a deal, but this was pretty offensive. "Just waive your right to a jury trial and we will give you some shiny beads" or some shit. Then I would have to deal with an incredulous prosecutor when I would just shrug and say we are going to trial on a silly matter. They take it personal, like it's all about me doubting they can convict the guy or wanting to cause them trouble. Sometimes that is a side benefit.

Mostly the prosecutors are just worried about somehow losing dumb cases and getting fired or winding up in misdemeanor court or whatever. So they get creepy intense about the whole thing, like winning a no-brainer is further evidence of greatness.

When it stopped being humorous and started being annoying I knew it was time to get out. The scheduling is what drove me to it. Having all those different judges who liked to schedule things at the same time combined with a bit of a depressive episode made a bit of a mess of things. So I'd have things sneak up on me. Plus there was some force at work that caused people to assume anything that came up was my problem.

For example, one morning I'm just lying in bed having a bit of an anxiety attack. The phone rings and it is Judge Conifer's secretary, a real sweetheart who operated on the assumption that every defendant and defense attorney are scum, asking me why I'm not there seeing as I have trial scheduled that morning.

I ask who the defendant is and she hangs up on me.

So I start to wonder how she knew my number. I call the office to ask if they might know what the fuck is going on. Meanwhile I'm getting dressed in a hurry and all of this is not helping the anxiety at all. Someone in the office finally admits to giving the number and gives me the name of the defendant. I've never heard of the person, but it was one of those names that was familiar enough to where there is that part of your mind that doesn't know for sure. So more worrying.

Turns out it was someone else's client. Someone left the office and I wound up with the lion's share of her cases, but not all. This was one of the few to go elsewhere, so it wasn't totally out to lunch that the staff assumed it was mine.

Still, it was jarring. It wasn't as weird as the time someone called me at the office (his was after hours and the switchboard was closed down) and asked me what the number was for the county prosecutor. Since somehow this person managed to get through to me in particular, via the extension list, I was curious as to why they were asking me this seeing it isn't a secret, and well, why me?

Simple answer. She was in Melbourne. No, not the one in Iowa. Australia. She did a net search, assumed that "Public Defender" was a sort of police, and well, picked me at random. I didn't ask why she needed the prosecutor. It was bound to be either anti-climatic or raise more questions than I wanted to ask back then.

Stuff like that seems to happen to me quite often, and good thing, too. It is a heck of a lot easier to write when reality is so screwed up that the only problem is that it doesn't exactly make for subtle fiction. I've written all of this stuff because I felt like I should, and probably will be as surprised and horrified as my High School English teachers if this huge pile of preposterous nonsense finds its way into print.

Prose therapy, more or less. I keep going back for more, mostly because I've managed to become semi-broke, but also because I'm curious if things can get any weirder.

They always do. I could have lost everything I own, which isn't much, betting on it.